WIN

LOSE

KILL

DIE

"A twisty, tricksy book that will leave you unable to trust anyone, including yourself. Ambition has never been so ruthless, school has never been so deadly."
Melinda Salisbury, author of _Hold Back the Tide_

"Once again Cynthia Murphy pulls me from a reading slump, pushes me to the edge of my seat, and has me racing through the pages to see who's still alive at the end. _WIN LOSE KILL DIE_ has all the spine-tingling terror of _LAST ONE TO DIE_ with even more stakes than ever before. A deliciously bloody read for all horror fans."
Melissa Welliver, author of _The Undying Tower_

"Cynthia Murphy cleverly weaves together teen drama and the dark side of ambition in this twisty thriller. _WIN LOSE KILL DIE_ will keep you up at night with its swoony romance, unpredictable mysteries and impressive body count. Witty, atmospheric and a little bit evil."
Kathryn Foxfield, author of _Good Girls Die First_

"An explosive, blood-thirsty thrill ride with a break-neck twist you'll be thinking about for days! Karen McManus fans will devour this."
Kat Ellis, author of _Harrow Lake_ and _Wicked Little Deeds_

"Perfect for fans of Truly Devious and 90s slasher movies, this twisty thriller has it all: a secret society steeped in intrigue, a deliciously creepy atmosphere and a plot that kept me guessing until the very end."
Amy McCaw, author of _Mina and the Undead_

"Deadly, twisted, and toxic. Cynthia Murphy is top of the class. I'd think twice about enrolling at Morton Academy."
Georgia Bowers, author of _Mark of the Wicked_

"_Win Lose Kill Die_ is deliciously dark and creepy and keeps you guessing the whole way through. Atmospheric and supremely murdery — I loved it!"
Julia Tuffs, author of _Hexed_

"I was hooked from the very first sentence. _Win Lose Kill Die_ is a thrilling mix of secret societies, murder and intrigue, making it one heck of a fun ride. A wickedly good book."
Josie Williams, author of _The Wanderer_

"With its breakneck pacing and twists that kept me guessing until the very end, _WIN LOSE KILL DIE_ ticked every box on my dark academia wish list: secret society, hooded cloaks, hidden passages, and of course, a relentless string of murders. I couldn't put it down!"
Brianna Bourne, author of _You & Me at the End of the World_

WIN ☐

LOSE ☐

KILL ☐

DIE ☒

CYNTHIA MURPHY

SCHOLASTIC

Published in the UK by Scholastic, 2022
1 London Bridge, London, SE1 9BG
Scholastic Ireland, 89E Lagan Road, Dublin Industrial Estate,
Glasnevin, Dublin, D11 HP5F

ISBN 978 0702 30494 1

A CIP catalogue record for this book
is available from the British Library.

Printed by CPI Group (UK) Ltd, Croydon, CR0 4YY
Paper made from wood grown in sustainable forests
and other controlled sources.

12

www.scholastic.co.uk

This one is for the godkids . . .

Kyla Somerville
Grayson Coffey
Dominic Kelly

. . . always remember to follow your dreams.

#

I didn't mean to kill the first one.

Honest.

It was just ... too easy, I suppose. She was already in the water, and when I plunged my hands in to help her out, I kind of ... changed my mind.

Something inside snapped.

I held Little Miss Perfect's head down and waited for her to stop thrashing around.

It took longer than I thought, and then she just ... floated there. Limp. Pathetic, really.

"Accidental death," according to the experts. That's nearly right. Like I said, it's not like I set out to do it.

It felt good, though.

2

I can't believe we're back here already.

Summer had passed by in a daze thanks to the bang to the head I took at the end of last term. Instead of going to beach parties with my friends and staying up to watch the sunrise like I planned, it was full of police interviews and PTSD. That last day of term had started so perfectly, and then. . .

"Liz." A sharp hiss and an elbow in my ribs bring me back to the present. Taylor is standing up straight, her gorgeous hazel eyes focused on the stage, for all the world playing the perfect mourner. I mimic her, my gaze following hers to a large easel draped in black cloth. It's displaying a large photograph of Morgan.

The girl who drowned in July.

"Pay attention." Taylor says this out of the corner of her mouth, like one of those creepy ventriloquist's puppets. She does it so effortlessly – not one muscle in her face moves. I guess I haven't recovered as well as I thought, even after all those hospital visits over the summer. I try to concentrate, I really do, but my mind wanders as the headmistress's words blur into one long sermon, each pause punctuated by the squeaking sound of rubber heels on the parquet floor. Autumn is seeping into the corners of the building already and the air smells of rain and damp, freshly laundered uniforms.

I study the picture. Morgan was pretty, in a preppy, Reese Witherspoon in *Cruel Intentions* kind of a way. She looked so sweet and unassuming, which I know was total bull. Truth is, Morgan had the personality of a venomous snake. You did *not* cross her, if you knew what was good for you; she'd make your life at Morton a total misery if she felt like it. It had been her idea to take the boat out on the lake that night, her big moment after being sworn in as head girl. She bullied most of us into it, from what I remember, though admittedly I don't remember much. Not after the boat flipped.

Dr Patel, the headmistress, ends her monologue with the request for a minute of silence. She's flanked by several members of the faculty – some of them are crying, dabbing handkerchiefs or tissues at their faces. Her sharp

3

black trouser suit is conservative, appropriate for a pupil's memorial, but super stylish and paired with some killer heels. I can't help but admire anyone who can walk in shoes that high, never mind run the country's most elite boarding school in them. The rest of the staff look frumpy in comparison. I watch the clock and sway slightly. I'm not used to standing up for so long after spending the summer in bed watching nineties movies.

Taylor ignores me, her head down, eyes closed: the perfect pupil. And mourner. Her long, naturally red hair falls like a curtain, spilling over the grey tweed of her blazer. Morton Academy's very own Cheryl Blossom, standing right next to me.

Dr Patel calls the memorial to a close and bodies start to shuffle towards the exit in silence.

"So," I whisper as we wait our turn to file out of the hall, "how does it feel?"

Taylor looks at me as we emerge through the tall, wooden doors into the corridor, smiling with her mouth but not her eyes. "How does what feel? Being passed over for head girl? Being so close to that full-ride scholarship I could practically taste it? Great, thanks for asking."

"Oh, come on. You're deputy! That's still pretty sweet. Plus" – I lower my voice, even though everyone else has resumed their own conversations too – "you know what that means for Jewel and Bone. Being deputy in the society means you get your pick of colleges."

4

Now the smile reaches her eyes.

"Yes, I do. I am very excited for this year. If I can just find the right sponsor, schmooze the right rich person, then I won't have to worry about working through university at all. Just think of all the people we're going to meet, the events we'll get to go to. . ."

"*You'll* get to go to," I correct her, smiling ruefully. "Some of the perks of the society don't stretch past head and deputy, remember?"

"Yeah, sorry." Taylor chews her lip and avoids my eyes. "I know that if you hadn't helped me and Kat with the scavenger hunt, you would have finished it before us. You'd be the one being sworn in as deputy head tonight and—"

"Hello, gorgeous!" A deep voice interrupts her as two heavy arms thump down around our shoulders. I'm kind of grateful for the interruption. Marcus's aftershave is so strong I start to cough, but Taylor immediately twinkles up at him. I duck out from under his arm and let them have a moment.

"What do you both look so serious about?" He looks good, like maybe he actually slept this summer. Lucky him.

"Oh, you know – life, death." She waves a polished hand in the air. "How I spent half an hour choosing a shade of lipstick that didn't clash with the funeral flowers." Taylor glances around furtively. "Actually, we were just talking about my ceremony at JB tonight." She stands on her tiptoes to kiss him. "You know your girl is going up in the world."

"I sure do. I still think you should've got the top spot instead of Jameela, though. I mean if there was anything I could do. . ." He walks out of the hall with us, but I stop listening as we start up the corridor to the entrance hall.

God, I missed this place. I breathe in deeply, as though I can inhale the pure essence of Morton into my very soul. I love the feeling of belonging, being one of a handful of kids from all over the country who are invited to attend such an exclusive sixth-form college. It doesn't matter who we are or where we're from – we're here because of our brains. Rich, poor, it doesn't matter at Morton. We're all here because we are damn clever – and the truth is that most of us wouldn't have got the chance otherwise. It's in the middle of nowhere and boarding is compulsory. There's no internet access without supervision, either – that's one of Morton's USPs: good old-fashioned bookwork. You win some, you lose some, I guess.

I take a second to remind myself it's all real. The stone ceiling soars over us, and our shoes tap softly on the ancient stone floor as we weave through bodies clad in grey blazers that are piped with an almost lurid acid green. The mahogany wall panels glow, sunlight streaming through the long windows that allow us glimpses of the vast, manicured gardens beyond them. We pass the headmistress's office and start to climb the large, curving staircase that always makes me feel like I'm in a Disney film. The handrail is gleaming, so polished that it's slick beneath my hand. The whole place smells of wood and citrus and I adore it. It smells like home.

"Hurry up, Liz." Marcus and Taylor are watching me with amusement from the landing above, and I realize I've zoned out a bit. "Stop daydreaming."

"Sorry." I duck my head to hide my flaming cheeks as I take the remaining stairs two at a time, until I reach the landing beneath a huge, stained-glass window. I walk slowly, following them through the huge double doors into the West Wing. Yes, I said West Wing – that's how big this place is.

This floor is all classrooms and the science labs are right next to classics, so I watch the perfect couple disappear into their room and then enter my own class. Classics is my main subject – we all do three in total, but we have been hand-selected for these ones in particular. It's kind of like a specialism, something we will take on to university, maybe even get fast-tracked. The teaching here is the best in the country – our expectations are set high. There's hardly anyone here yet, the assembly has interfered with the timetable for the first full day back, so I choose a desk in the middle row, by a window that looks out on to a wide expanse of water.

The lake.

Morgan.

I move quickly, my flesh crawling as memories of that night once again try to claw their way to the surface. I take a pew at the opposite side of the room, as far from the window as I can get.

The classroom fills up slowly and I'm pleased we have a small group – not that we ever have large classes, with only fifty chosen to attend Morton in each year group. The teacher arrives last and I'm pleased to see we've got Professor Insoll again. The man's a legend – in the world of ancient religious artefacts, anyway. He used to teach at degree level but I guess Morton pays pretty well – plus it has to be a bonus when you have a bunch of kids who are desperate to learn rather than perpetually hungover undergrads.

We go through all the usual first-day-back motions – new textbooks, a prep schedule that looks ridiculously full, and a winter exam timetable. I'm busy writing my name on everything when a note slides across my desk.

"Pass this to Jameela," a voice hisses.

Jameela? Hmm. I wonder if it's Jewel and Bone business, maybe a note about the first of the donor meetings, where we'll get to meet prospective sponsors who will hopefully pay our way through university, but a quick glance around reveals hardly anyone else in the class would have that kind of information. I shrug and pass it on to Frank, just in case it is. I can't go handing out potential secret society information to just anybody. "For Jameela," I mouth, nodding to the girl with long, dark braids sitting in front of him. I go back to signing my name with a flourish and forget all about the note.

Until Jameela shoots out of her seat, screaming, and drops the paper like it's on fire.

3

"Then what happened?"

"Nothing." I shrug. Taylor hoots a laugh, though there's not much humour in it.

"Trust Jameela to get away with making such a scene," she grumbles. "How did Insoll not confiscate the note?"

"She hid it pretty quickly, told him there was a spider on her desk."

We fall silent for a moment and I enjoy the sound of the gravel driveway crunching beneath my new shoes as we walk away from the main school building. I glance back, watching it get smaller and smaller, its myriad windows reflecting the late afternoon sun in a hundred different directions.

I divert my attention back to the path and smile over at Taylor, irresistibly reminded of the first time we walked this way. We're still in our uniforms, a JB requirement, and the stiff wool of my pleated skirt tickles my bare legs with every step as I try to keep up with her.

"She looked pretty shaken up," I say. "I wish I knew what it said. Why didn't I look at it? I mean, I was holding it!"

"Because you're Liz Williams, the nicest girl in all of Morton." The main gates into the grounds, large, metal things that hide us away from the real world, have come into our line of sight, so Taylor veers off to the left. We switch the driveway for the manicured lawn and head towards a dense copse of trees. She's right, of course. I am nice.

"Boring, right?" I say. She pauses and turns back to me, linking her arm through my own.

"Never." She grins, bumping my hip. "You're my moral compass, Lizzy. What would I do without you? Besides, it was probably just another of her nudes from last year."

She has a point, on both counts.

"Come on," I sigh. "We don't want to be late for this."

"Agreed." Taylor drops my arm as we approach a thickly wooded section of the grounds. She holds open a small wooden gate as I take one last glance around for any stragglers. The long, sweeping driveway is clear, Morton House tiny in the distance. It's almost seven, so everyone else will be doing prep after dinner. Perfect. We both ignore the "No Entry" sign hammered into the flaking wood – it's not for us, after all – and within seconds the darkness of the trees has enveloped us.

It was last summer when I had first realized this part of the grounds even existed, after the riddles had appeared on our pillows and we followed the clues that had been scattered around the building. No one really comes out this way, which is kind of the point, I guess. The rest of the grounds here are so picture-perfect: grass always cut, flowerbeds freshly dug, hedges pruned. This bit is wild, fairy tale forest-like, full of snapping twigs and tiny, scampering feet. As if on cue, a squirrel appears in front of us, his bushy tail twitching in time with his tiny nose, ears pricked and alert. He eyes us bravely but scarpers the second we move.

"Aww, cute!" I whisper.

"Why are you whispering?" Taylor whispers back.

"Why are *you* whispering?" I giggle. She rolls her eyes at me but the laughter is contagious and a smile starts to tug at the corner of her mouth.

"Stop it," she whispers back and we both dissolve into silent laughter. It's the nerves, it must be. Last time we were all here was *that* night.

The laughter dies in my throat.

"Hey." Taylor pauses. I'm sure she can read my mind sometimes. "How are you feeling? Are you ready for this?"

"Yes." My voice comes out as intended, firm and unwavering, though I'm not sure I *am* ready. Taylor reaches out a hand and for a second my vision blurs and it's hers, Morgan's, reaching desperately from the black water.

Then it's just Taylor's hand again, nails perfectly manicured, not blue and dripping lake moss. I stare until she drops it and sighs.

"Come on then. Like you said, we can't be late – you know what she thinks about starting on time. I don't know about you, but I want to be charming all those rich donors once we start meeting them. I heard a rumour that two girls from last year were so late to a meeting that they were stuck serving canapés during their first sponsorship party as punishment..."

We delve deeper into the trees and I keep my head down, away from the low hanging branches that threaten to tangle bony fingers in my hair. The path is narrow here, fringed with wild orchids that are taller than both of us. Their dark purple tongues leer as we pass and they stink of decay, a sickly sweet odour that burrows into your nostrils and doesn't go away. We should have taken the other path, the one that's maintained, but that would have brought us past the lake and I don't want to deal with that until I have to. I realize Taylor has bought me this way on purpose – she knows I'm avoiding the lake. I thank her silently.

The area ahead of us begins to widen and I can just make out glimpses of roughly hewn grey stone through the brush. Brambles have been left to go wild here and my brain dredges up a memory of an old DVD I would watch on repeat, when the witch curses Sleeping Beauty and the thorns surround the princess's castle. These ones are almost welcoming, though, the way they have woven together, arching over us to create an entrance of sorts. We duck our heads and pass through, then follow the short stone path to an ancient wooden doorway where we pause for breath.

"Ready?" I whisper.

Taylor straightens her shoulders and nods once. "Ready."

We push open the door which, despite its obvious antiquity, is well oiled and guides us into the chapel in silence. It's dark inside and the thick walls immediately muffle any sounds of the outside world. We close the door gently and give our eyes a second to adjust to the flickering candlelight at the opposite end of the aisle. You'd almost think it was a fully working church, not a front for something else. I guess that's kind of the point.

I follow Taylor down the aisle and pause in front of the altar, my good girl Catholic school upbringing making me drop a knee and bow my head quickly, before catching her up at another wooden door. This one is behind the altar, where the priest would usually go at the end of mass. We pass through it in silence and it feels wrong, like it usually does, but I remind myself it's not a *real* church and keep my head down as we walk past the others. We stop at the far end of the room, in front of one of the wooden benches that line the walls. My mind flashes back to the last time I was in here, snatches of memory seeping in. Puddles of lake water on the worn stone floor. Morgan, her blank face, lips blue...

I shake my head, hard. No. Not now. The doctor warned me this might happen once I came back to Morton, but I didn't expect so many flashbacks so soon.

I shrug off my blazer, hang it carefully on a peg and run my fingers over the small, gem-encrusted pin that's attached to the inside pocket, the one that sits over my heart. I smile as I remember finding it on my pillow, its sharp spike pushed through the paper that invited me to the hunt. I take a second to smooth down my skirt and make sure my shirt is tucked in neatly, not that anyone will see it. Only then do I pick up the long, folded gown from the bench and slide it over my head. I remove the little skull-shaped pin from my blazer. The sharpness of the gemstones prick against my fingers as I fasten it on to my cloak. The thick velvet flows down over me, swallowing my uniform and pooling around my feet. I brush my hair back and tuck it behind my ears, pulling the hood up and over so it sits low, casting a large, hollow shadow where my face should be. I glance at Taylor, now hidden behind an identical robe, before following her and half a dozen other figures down the staircase that is hidden in a shadowed corner.

To the crypt.

I trail the dark procession to the bottom step and, as usual, I am the last one. I wait as everyone else takes their positions and, when it's my turn, I step out on to a narrow platform. I am standing on a raised stone pathway that forms a circle, more paths spiking off towards the centre, so from above they would look like the spokes of a wheel. My robe, always too long, drags in the inches of floodwater below and cold fingers spread up through the velvet as though they are clawing at my ankles. I shake the thought from my head and finally arrive at my plinth, taking my place in the circle.

I try my best to ignore the dead body in the centre.

I keep my head down, so I'm cocooned in my own little world of velvet and icy cold. Around me the air gradually stills, shuffles of feet and whispers of swishing robes quieting down as the rest of the group settles into their positions. Only when the room is silent do I allow myself to look up and focus my eyes on the stone plinth in the middle.

I won't lie – the first time I saw Old Josef, I was pretty freaked out. I'd just trekked through the woods, following the final clue in the library – a small, jewel-coloured chapel wrought into one of the stained-glass windows. When you stand at a certain angle, at the right time, the sun shines through and practically points at this part of the woods. The clues in the hunt had all been so cryptic – kind of the point, I guess, so not everyone could solve them – but I'd worked my way through them, dropping hints for Kat and Taylor, who had both received riddles too. When I found the chapel they were there as well. I let them go in ahead of me, not quite realizing what it would mean, and we followed the music down into the crypt. We weren't the first ones there. I was handed a robe and led to my place – there were five others ahead of us – while we waited for the rest of the platforms to fill up.

When the room was full and we took off our hoods, it was explained to us that this revealed the hierarchy of the society. Marcus had been the first male to arrive and, out of the girls, Morgan was in the top spot. They were sworn in as head girl and boy immediately, along with their deputies, and the rest of us became prefects. I would have been slightly higher in the pecking order if I hadn't let Taylor and Kat in before me.

I refocus on the present and narrow my eyes at Old Josef again. The more you look at him, the more fascinating he becomes. He rests in his coffin of glass, like some twisted, medieval version of Snow White, and has been there for as long as Morton has been a school. Some people say he came from Poland, others Germany, though all that is left of him now is in this casket, so we'll likely never know either way. He was some kind of saint, apparently, who ended up here when the school's founder needed something new and eccentric for his cabinet of curiosities.

My eyes travel along the skeleton, and I imagine trailing my fingers along the rough, golden brocade that wraps around each individual rib, the central panel of fabric encrusted with precious stones that decorates his sternum and the magnificent collar that envelops his bony neck. His face hangs open in a rictus grin and the top of his skull is encircled by a glorious crown of hand-carved crystals, all wired together with gold. His skeletal hands are beringed and rest gently on his stomach – or where his stomach would be, I guess. His bottom half is out of sight, draped in moth-eaten velvet and shadows.

"Bow to our hallowed companion, in honour of our founder."

I do it automatically, following the instructions of the disembodied voice, as though the words themselves curl around my spine and push me gently forwards at the waist. The words echo around the room and I dip my upper body forwards in as deep a bow as I can manage without falling into the water below. Once I straighten up, I glance at Old Josef once more and whisper the same words as everyone else in the room, though this time they are directed at the grave that lays below his casket. The final resting place of Patrick Morton, founder and first headmaster of Morton Academy. The man who decided he would help the *really* clever kids succeed by matching them with people who would pay for their educations. He's kind of a Jewel and Bone hero. "Thank you, founder. We honour you with jewels and remember you with bone. May we succeed."

"Acolyte Asanti, step forward," the voice calls and I pinpoint its location to the plinth that would be at twelve, if this were a clock. The figure in Jameela's spot glides forwards on the narrow stone ledge that connects the outer circle to the inner sanctum. As soon as she steps on to the island that holds the bones of our founder, another command is given. "Remove your hood."

Jameela is pretty and petite, and the cloak swamps her more than most. Taylor must be gutted. Jameela was the second girl to complete the hunt so she's been promoted from deputy and now has the pick of any university she wants to go to. Like *any*: Oxford, Harvard, UCLA. She can walk right in and the whole thing is covered. I allow myself to daydream for a second, imagining attending classes at Yale or Cambridge, all paid for. No student loans, no term-time jobs.

I refocus and watch intently as Jameela removes her hood. To be fair to her, the girl is clever – she was plucked from some nowhere town as some kind of mathematical genius. I hate maths, too many numbers, too much logic – I much prefer the history of people, delving into the reasons behind the beauty they have created and left behind, whether it's in artwork, architecture or just good old stories. I think it's why I was so smitten at the idea of a secret society – it's like stepping into an as-yet-unwritten part of history.

Jameela's smooth skin gleams golden in the flickering candlelight but she is biting her lip. She looks nervous and I just know that Taylor is screaming on the inside. She would never allow herself to show fear. She would appear brimming with poise and confidence even if she didn't feel it.

Especially if she didn't.

"Acolyte Asanti, do you dutifully ascend to the coveted position of head girl? A role that will not only afford you status within Morton Academy and beyond, but also within the Society of Jewel and Bone."

Jameela clears her throat. "Yes. I do."

"Then may you succeed."

"May you succeed," I repeat with the rest of the group. It feels like a lifetime ago that we stood here doing the same ritual for Morgan, but it has only been weeks. Six to be exact. Maybe that's why Jameela looks so worried – does she think the position is cursed?

"Acolyte Fox, step forward."

Here we go – this is how it should be done. Even in her gown, Taylor strides down the narrow path like a supermodel and takes the place next to her superior. She drops her hood and even from here I can see the sparkle in her eyes, the perfect flick of her eyeliner. I stand a little straighter, proud to be watching her. She's a natural.

"Acolyte Fox, do you respectfully ascend to the position of deputy head girl? A role that will not only afford you status within Morton Academy and beyond, but also within the Society of Jewel and Bone?"

"Yes, I do."

"Then may you succeed."

"May you succeed," I say, through a smile. I want to applaud but the most important part is coming.

"Are you both ready to swear your blood oath?"

"We are." The girls clasp hands and the figure who has been speaking breaks away from their platform and joins them in the centre. A shining, silver blade slides from an oversized sleeve and is presented to Jameela, who I swear goes a little grey; after all, she's done this once before, when she was sworn in as deputy last summer.

Taylor keeps her head held high as Jameela takes the knife. It's an old blade, as old as the body they are flanking I'd guess, and just as encrusted in jewels. The blade is kept sharp, though, something that is evident as Jameela slices into her own palm, and then Taylor's upturned one. They both step towards the skeleton and, as the glass case is opened for them, they each lightly grasp an arm bone, smearing their blood upon the blood of hundreds of previous pledges. On top of Morgan's.

"Esteemed acolytes, please welcome the new head and

22

deputy head girl of the Society of Jewel and Bone. As you know, this grants you the same esteemed positions within Morton Academy. Many congratulations."

Applause and a loud whoop from someone who can only be Marcus echoes around the cavern and I join in enthusiastically. That feeling of belonging floods through me again, and I remember how intoxicating it can be. No matter what happens outside these walls, this place right here is mine. I am part of something special. Something important.

Jameela and Taylor embrace and the third figure removes her own hood, a shiny sheet of hair swishing as Dr Patel, the headmistress of Morton, kisses each girl twice, once on each cheek. She then turns to the crowd and holds up one hand, a signal to silence our applause and remove our hoods. I tear mine off like a doctor pulling off a mask after a seventeen-hour surgery and relish the tickle of the cold air on the sweaty nape of my neck. The space to my left is empty, meaning Kat hasn't arrived back yet. I hope she doesn't get in trouble for missing the first meeting.

"Welcome back, acolytes." Dr Patel gestures around the room with the blade she has retrieved from Jameela, before it disappears back into her robes, still blood-stained and dripping. "Our first meeting of the year is usually brief, given that it is the first day back. Tonight, however, we had to undertake the somewhat unusual task of welcoming a new pair into the hierarchy. Thankfully our head boy and deputy are both present and well." Dr Patel nods towards Marcus and Frank, respectively. They nod back. "Now that is over, I will proceed as normal, and ask the traditional question of our new head girl and the head boy." She turns to face Jameela, who holds a thick, bloodied piece of gauze to her left palm. "First, Acolyte Asanti, do you have any business you would like to discuss with the group?"

"Yes." Jameela's answer is a shock and, judging by the whispers around the room, not only to me. What could she have to discuss so soon?

The note?

"I see." Dr Patel's voice is hard to read, as usual. That woman gives nothing away. "Well, the floor is yours."

"Thank you." Jameela looks less nervous and more terrified as she pulls a piece of paper from within her robes. She clears her throat. "I got this today."

It *is* the note. I lean forward a little.

"I didn't want to believe it but I don't think we can ignore it." She hands the crumpled paper to Dr Patel, who reads it with an inscrutable expression.

"It could be a sick joke," she says to Jameela.

"It could," she agrees, "but Morgan was my best friend. I think we should take it seriously."

"Very well." Dr Patel hands the paper back to her. "You may address the group."

Jameela swallows hard and holds the crumpled paper

aloft. The room is swathed in silence. "It's . . . it's a photo. Of Morgan, from her memorial." I strain to hear as her voice drops. "With her eyes scratched out." There's a collective intake of breath as she clears her throat and reads aloud from the page in her hand.

"Morgan's death was not an accident. I killed her.
And you're next."

5

The looks on their faces when she pulled out that photograph! I could not have planned it any better. I didn't expect her to take it so seriously, though. Let alone make it public. I thought it would just make Miss-look-at-me-I'm-the-new-head-girl squirm.

In hindsight it was arrogant of me. I just couldn't help it. It's getting hard to suppress the urge to do whatever I want. To tell the whole truth, officer, it's getting hard to suppress the urge to do a lot of things.

So, what now? I suppose there's no way I can let her start investigating, especially not with the whole society behind her. Though that might be fun ... it was such a bad idea to share it with everyone there tonight. Such a bad idea — I had only intended to scare her. Maybe make her drop out. I wasn't going to do anything. . . bad.

Oh, who am I kidding. Of course I was intending to do something bad.

So, Jameela. Target number two.

"What do you think?"

I tear my eyes away from my battered copy of *The Secret History* and frown at Taylor. Some people think reading equals doing nothing and love to interrupt right when you get to the juiciest parts.

I cast an only slightly interested eye over Taylor's outfit from my cross-legged position on the bed. The first day of term traditionally ends with a pyjama party on the roof for seniors, and our long hallway is full of girls laughing, running in and out of each other's rooms and posing in their best PJs. I should have known my Fair Isle leggings and oversized hoody wouldn't cut it. I wasn't able to work this summer, thanks to my head injury, so I'm stuck with last year's stuff.

Taylor is wearing a silky ivory two-piece: short shorts trimmed with black piping and lace and a fitted, long-sleeved button-down shirt, the cuffs open and rolled up to her elbows. Her name is embroidered over a pocket on her chest and the remains of a summer tan on her legs contrasts beautifully.

"Those must have cost a bomb! Don't tell me you waitressed all summer just so you could spend it all on new clothes for second year?"

"Of course I did." She sighs. "I saved all of my tips for day trips, though – we should be let out of this place every month this year. I just wanted to look good, you know?" Her voice shrinks. "And now it's even more important. I need to look deputy head girl worthy."

"You look amazing," I reassure her as I look down at my own chest, where *"Do Not Disturb – Duvet Day in Progress"* is emblazoned. Taylor flips her immaculately straightened hair over one shoulder and pouts down at me. I missed her over the summer, more than I thought I would. Thank God for FaceTime.

"Thanks. And you look super cute! So cosy – I think I'll freeze up there."

"You'll have Marcus to keep you warm."

"I know." A wicked smile crosses her face as she leans down to look in the mirror on her bedside table. I take the opportunity to carry on reading. "Are we going to get you a little plaything this year?"

"Oh, stop." I close the book, defeated, and watch as she layers another slick of gloss across full lips. "I've got enough on this year without boys getting involved. Anyway, they all kind of suck and I am not trawling the juniors for new blood."

"OK, OK." She holds up her blusher brush in defeat. "Consider me told ... ouch! What the hell?"

"What is it?"

Taylor puts the brush at arm's length and checks her face in the mirror again. "Something sharp in my brush, it just scratched me."

"Seriously? Let me see." I hold a hand out for the brush and she shoves it at me, patting the skin of her cheekbone gingerly.

"Ugh, that stings. What is it?"

I study the bristles and pull out the offending object. "Here's the culprit." I wince, holding up a small, rusty nail. "How did that get in there?"

"Eww, gross! Who knows, it's not exactly designer. One day I will have decent stuff, I swear." She paints on a smile, straightens up and slips her feet into black fluffy sliders. "Can you see the scratch?"

"No," I answer honestly. "Not a thing."

"Good." She wiggles her eyebrows at me. "Ready?"

I unfold myself and swing my legs off the bed, pushing my feet into battered rubber flip-flops.

"Ready," I agree.

The hallway has pretty much emptied out now, the last girls trailing up the spiral staircase in the corner of the corridor, footsteps echoing on the iron. We start to follow them up to the lounge but Taylor stops me.

"Here," she hisses, thrusting a small glass bottle my way. "Keep hold of that, will you? I've got some mixers upstairs."

Vodka. I haven't drunk since last summer term. My stomach turns just thinking about it.

"No chance." I thrust it back but she steps away. "Taylor, you know I'm not supposed to drink on my meds. I could have a seizure."

"I know, you don't have to. I just need you to hide it in your jumper, please? Just 'til we get on the roof." She gestures at her flimsy pyjamas and sticks her bottom lip out in another pout. "I don't have anywhere to hide it."

"Fine," I huff, shoving the cold bottle into the kangaroo pouch on my jumper. "But only because it's for you. I am not getting caught with this and I am not helping you drink it, OK?"

"Of course." She beams at me and catches hold of my hand, giving it a squeeze. "Thank you. Now, let's start this year off right!"

Taylor skips over to the spiral staircase and begins to bound up it as I follow, careful not to drop the glass bottle on the metal steps.

*

31

The lounge is packed with girls from our year, most of them wearing some variation of Taylor's outfit matched with pristine hair and make-up. I touch my own sleek bob and slide my fingers into the patch where the staples had been. The hair there is rough and bristly from being shaved and growing back in the weirdest ways. I wish it was long again, but my head injury last summer didn't leave me with much choice but to cut it short.

"Lizzie!" A loud squeal shakes me from my self-pity as strong arms crush my shoulders from behind. "God, you're skin and bone! How the hell are you?"

"Hey, Kat," I squeak. She releases me and I turn around to give my friend a big squeeze. "I was wondering when I'd see you. I didn't see your stuff in the room."

"Literally just got back from Cyprus this morning, we had a family wedding. I've been travelling all day, walked through the door about five minutes ago, so I just dumped it and followed the noise."

"I can tell – you're so tanned! You look amazing, as usual."

"I spent the summer at the gym." She flexes one bare arm and I see muscle there that would put most of the lads to shame. "You should come with me now we're back." She squeezes my own arm through the thin hoody and I wince. "It'd be good for you, like rehab or something."

"Er, yeah, maybe." She grins at me; she knows full well I have no intention of going with her. "Hey, come say hi to Taylor. We have got to fill you in on what you have already missed."

We weave through the room as I regale her with the events of the day: the memorial, Jameela's note in classics class and, finally, the JB meeting.

"Wait." She stops and stares at me. "Someone is claiming they killed Morgan? Seriously? Who knows about this?"

"Only the other acolytes, I think." I shrug. "Jameela was pretty freaked out, anyway."

"Did Patel take it seriously?"

"Hard to tell," I muse. "She doesn't give much away."

"True. What does Taylor think?" Kat asks.

"Not sure. I reckon she thinks Jameela is playing up, looking for attention. She's still a bit sore on Jameela automatically being sworn in as head girl. She thought there'd be some sort of new challenge or something, so she could prove herself. Don't tell her I said that, though!"

Kat shakes her head. "Of course I won't. I wonder if it's ever happened before. Someone not finishing the year as head girl."

"I dunno. Maybe Taylor's right. I mean Jameela is a bit of a drama queen."

"This is true. Come on, enough morbid talk for now. I need a drink and to see if Caroline is still wearing that crop top she loved so much last year..."

"Perv," I giggle. We start moving again and I try my

33

best to soak up the atmosphere. Seniors at Morton, finally. God, I dreamed of this last year. There were always whispers of parties and I never thought I'd finally be at one, but here I am, a Jewel and Bone acolyte, no less.

I take in as much of my surroundings as I can. It's not that different to our lounge from last year but the excitement in the air is real. There's a whole dark academia vibe to the room: age-worn leather armchairs and wooden-panelled walls. One whole side of the room is decorated with miniature portraits of head girls gone by, Dr Patel among them. Morgan's picture is up on the wall already – no matter how brief her reign, if it happened at Morton you could bet it would be documented. The photographs go all the way back to 1906, when the Academy was founded, and I suddenly feel queasy with the eyes of a hundred more girls on me.

"Lizzie?" Kat is staring at me, concern in her eyes. "Are you feeling all right?" Her thick Northern accent is soft.

"Yeah, yeah, of course. Just being a space cadet. Sorry – just a side effect, you know?" I rub the bristles over my scar.

"OK." She doesn't look convinced. "You'll be fine, I promise. We've got you."

"I know. Thanks, Kat. Now come on, this vodka Taylor made me carry is burning a hole through my conscience. I need to get rid."

We approach the back of the room, where two huge

balcony doors provide a view of the countryside for miles around. A small kitchen area in the corner comes into view and, sure enough, Taylor's there, rummaging around in the tiny fridge. She stands up, triumphantly brandishing a bottle of Diet Coke, half of which she promptly pours down the sink.

"Vodka?"

"Vodka." I slide the bottle out and hand it to her. We close ranks, Kat on one side, me on the other, as she pours it into the Coke bottle.

"Voila!" She gives it a swirl and takes a swig. My own mouth waters, my stomach turning just thinking of the sting but, as ever, Taylor's face doesn't give anything away. "Right," she shouts to the room of girls, "now I'm ready to party!"

"Did someone say party?" A thick Essex accent interrupts and the room falls silent as Jameela emerges from her room. That is a definite perk of being chosen as head girl – your own room on the top floor, own bathroom, everything. Another reason Taylor's jealous – imagine not having to queue for the shower? "Seniors, are we ready to welcome the new school year?"

A chorus of *"hell yeah"* fills the room as Jameela squares her shoulders and glides through the crowd, flanked by her old room-mates, Emily and Ayesha. They smile and nod, and Emily pats the place over her heart as she passes me, where her JB pin would be, a gesture from one acolyte to

35

another. I return the gesture.

A shiny black badge decorates the lapel of Jameela's pyjamas, which are a deep, dark red that perfectly matches her lipstick. She strolls towards the balcony doors, the one thing our junior lounge did *not* have, and flings them open, a soft, late summer breeze filtering into the room.

"Seniors" – she smiles – "I declare this year officially open for business."

7

The roof garden is *gorgeous,* even more so in the dying light of late evening. Last year, when we were in the junior lounge, we used to stare out of the windows and wish we could come out here. I think a couple of the maths girls tried once, but as far as I know, it did not end well for them.

The walls that enclose the roof garden are magical, castle-like crenelations, just high enough to see over. There's fake grass underfoot, so I kick off my flip-flops and let the blades tickle and scratch the soles of my feet as I pad over to peek at the view.

Nothing but acres and acres of fields surround us, a

patchwork quilt of lavender fields, densely knotted pockets of woodland and a hundred shades of green. I turn back to the terrace. Tiny bistro tables and chairs are dotted around, each a different vibrant colour, yellows and pinks and peacock shades of teal and violet. Long strings of solar lightbulbs arch overhead, anchored on the walls and all sweeping up to join together on a flagpole that juts ceremoniously from the centre of the building, giving the illusion of a skeletal circus tent. Tiny, flickering tealights have been placed into plant pots and these line the long wooden benches that cling to the inner side of the walls. I take a deep breath and turn to smile at Kat and Taylor. They grin back – I think Taylor might even be a little teary-eyed. Not that she'd show weakness in front of all these people.

"Come on." She swigs from her bottle again and marches through the roof garden, turning the corner around the junior lounge.

Our side of the terrace is an upside-down L-shape, so once you're around the corner, you can't see our lounge any more. We *can* see the other side, though: a mirror image of our own.

The boys' side.

Morton is totally old school when it comes to sleeping arrangements, even though all of the lessons and extra-curriculars are mixed. The girls' dorms and lounges are in the West Wing and the boys' are in the East. From what little Taylor tells me, the layout is pretty much the same over there. Out here, though, in front of the flagpole and directly between the wings, there's a wall to separate us.

Well, it tries to.

Marcus, of course, is the first one over. The wall itself is low but there's a tall, metal fence on top of it, capped with spikes. There's no way to climb it and, even if you did, getting skewered by one of those would mean a definite trip to the infirmary – and how were you going to explain that one? Marcus doesn't even attempt it. Instead, he hoists himself on to the crenelated outer wall, swings a leg around the edge and sits there, one leg either side of the metal pole. His large hands are wrapped around the end fence post, letting it take his weight.

I swear you can hear the collective intake of breath from forty-nine other kids as his body hangs over the four-storey drop.

"Yes, Marcus!" Someone shouts from the lads' side, and others start to join in, chanting his name. If I didn't know Taylor so well, I'd say she wasn't bothered about the fact her boyfriend was risking his life to climb over the wall, but I'm close enough to see faint tension lines around her mouth. I reach down and squeeze her hand but her eyes stay fixed on him as he swings his other leg over. She doesn't let her breath out until both feet are firmly planted on this side of the wall. Then she takes a huge swig from her bottle.

"Easy." Marcus shrugs, turning to look at the crowd of girls before him. His eyes land on Taylor and he points at her. "There she is," he booms, "the only girl I'd risk my life for."

"Oh, please," she says, but her tension has melted away and she laughs as everyone bursts into heckles around us. She saunters over and I feel that familiar tug of longing in my chest as she smiles up at him. Not jealousy, exactly, but a definite ache of . . . something.

The party starts to erupt around us. The rest of the boys follow Marcus's lead and pretty soon the whole of the senior class is crammed on to our side of the roof garden and drinks start to appear from ever more innovative places. I look around for Kat and see she's already doing some kind of push-up competition with the lads from the football team so take a wide berth around *that* and stop to say hi to Frank and some of the other kids from my history class.

That's when I see him.

Now, I'm not the most dramatic person ever, but for a second I swear that the noise dulls a little, the crowd parts ever so slightly and everything moves in slow-motion. I know every student in our year group and I've never seen this one before. He's tall and slim, taller than me, and his skin is light brown. He cracks a smile and I see the most amazing set of teeth outside of Netflix. I'm staring, I know I am, but I can't help it. A small group surrounds him over in the far corner of the garden, right by the corner wall, and it takes me a second to realize that Taylor and Marcus are part of that group. In fact, Tay is waving at me and from the look on her face, it's clear that she hasn't just started. I hustle over.

"Hey," she says, shooting me a meaningful look as I join the group. "We were just talking about you, weren't we, Marcus?"

"What? Oh, yeah. Hey, Liz, meet Cole. He's just started."

"Hey." Cole nods at me and up close I can see that he is, in fact, one of the best-looking people I have *ever* met. He's wearing these loose, black trousers and a high-necked shirt made from the same type of material. Linen, I think. It has those little buttons on it, at the throat and cuffs, and I wonder if it's some kind of martial-arts uniform.

"Not quite," he laughs and I realize I've just voiced my thoughts aloud again. Damn it, I really need to watch that particular side effect of my medication; it could get me in a lot of trouble. Especially while he's around.

"Sorry, I didn't mean because you were. . ."

"What, Chinese?" He laughs again. "Don't worry. Nah, they do look like something out of *Cobra Kai* but they're my honest-to-god PJs." He holds up two fingers in defence of his story, the rest of his fingernails pink from the pressure of his long fingers holding a green glass bottle.

"They are from my Cantonese grandma, though. Hong Kong specials. Think they cost her about three quid on Mong Kok market."

"Oh." Oh? Is that all I've got? My cheeks heat up. I'm literally feeling myself blush, right in his face.

"Yeah." He takes a swig of his beer and holds it out to me. "Want some?"

"No, thanks, I don't drink."

He grins at me and takes another swig. "Sensible. Interesting."

Seriously, how much blood do my cheeks need right now?

"Hey." Taylor nudges me and nods towards a small group by the central wall. "Look." A couple of the boys have climbed back over and disappeared inside and now they emerge with a small box in tow, which they pass through the metal railings to the group on our side. A red-clad arm reaches out to grab it – Jameela and entourage. From the look of her, she's wasted already. I wonder if they were drinking in her new room since after the meeting. I check my watch – they must have been, we've only been out here half an hour.

"Smoking." I wrinkle my nose. "Gross."

"I'm surprised Jameela is even entertaining it," Taylor snorts. "Doesn't she have really bad asthma? Maybe being head girl has literally gone to her head."

"It could be the note?" I suggest. "She seemed to take

that pretty seriously. Doesn't smoking calm your nerves or something?"

"Eww, no, that's such a myth. Oh well, sucks for her." Taylor's eyes narrow for a second, but I blink and the expression is gone, as if I imagined it. "Anyway," she chirps, smiling pointedly in my direction, "Cole, tell us all about you. . ."

A loud, spluttering cough interrupts just as he opens his pretty mouth, and the rooftop falls silent. Jameela is doubled over by the railings, drawing loud, hacking breaths that sound painful, raw.

"For the love of..." Marcus breaks away from us and moves over to her, quickly tailed by Taylor.

Cole looks at me in confusion.

"What's happening?"

"I don't know."

We follow the crowd. Jameela is now on her knees, both hands on the ground, trying desperately to calm her breathing, though I can see the fear in her eyes from here. Her friends stand around stupidly, only Emily having the sense to pat her on the back. Jameela weakly pushes her away and tries to get to her feet. I spot Marcus running towards the lounge from the corner of my eye. What's he doing? Getting water?

"For God's sake!" Taylor yells. "The girl has asthma. Does she have an inhaler?"

"Er, yeah, I think so. . ." Ayesha splutters, looking

around with tears in her eyes. "I mean, she should. I think it's in her room; I knew where it was in our dorm last year but she moved everything, so. . ."

"I've got it." Marcus pushes back through the crowd and shoves a small, pink piece of plastic into Taylor's hand. "It should help, my sister has the same one."

"Jameela?" Taylor's voice is firm but clear, like she's talking to a toddler. Jameela looks up, one hand at her throat, her breath ragged and wheezing. You can hear how sore and inflamed her throat is; the air is almost whistling through it. "Jameela? Take this. Two puffs, OK?"

Jameela grabs the inhaler and forces it into her mouth, pressing the button and taking a deep, rattling breath. Her shoulders relax slightly and she exhales and takes another, the panic clearing from her eyes. She keeps the inhaler in her mouth and takes a noticeably deeper breath, using her free hand to give the crowd a shaky thumbs up, before dropping the medicine and pulling a face. It clearly tastes awful.

"Good old Taylor," I say, turning back to Cole who looks as shell-shocked as I feel. "She's always calm in a crisis."

"Jeez." He throws back the rest of his drink. "Think I need another one of these. Come on."

I follow him back to the corner of the rooftop as the crowd around the railings breaks up and the party slowly recovers. We sit cross-legged on a load of cushions that have been piled in the corner, our backs to the wall. "That was crazy. Is it always so eventful at Morton?"

I flash back to the last day of summer term as he grabs another bottle. Taking the boat out that night, the panic as it flipped. Morgan, cold and still as Taylor gave her CPR and I drifted in and out of consciousness. The rest of the newly minted acolytes huddled around, useless, just like tonight. Emily and Ayesha hadn't been able to help their friend then, either. Dr Patel on the phone, barking orders at the boys, only Marcus actually up and doing something. . .

"No," I say. "Nothing much ever happens here—"

My lie is split by a scream.

"Jameela? JAMEELA?!"

For the final time that evening, silence descends on the party as Emily screams her friend's name over and over. Even from here, through a tangle of legs, I can see a body on the ground, one hand clasped around her throat. Jameela is still, hunched over in the foetal position, lying on the floor. She doesn't look right.

"Liz? Is she. . ." Cole's voice is tinged with panic.

"No," I breathe. "No, she's just . . . she's just. . ."

I trail off as Frank kneels down next to Jameela and takes her pulse, first in her neck, then grabbing her wrist as he tries to time her heartbeats on his watch. He places her arm down gently before shaking his head.

Another head girl, dead.

Well.

That was certainly unexpected.

I was happy to let them enjoy the party tonight, but silly little Jameela had to try and be all cool and grown-up, didn't she? I was hoping she'd take the inhaler before bed and pop off quietly, make it look more natural. I can't believe she didn't taste the camphor – she must have been drunk. Getting hold of her inhaler was hardly a challenge either, I was able to stroll right into her room in plain sight today. But this – well, this was much more exciting.

I guess the ads are right – smoking really can kill.

"Here." I drape the comforter over Taylor's shoulder and she grabs it gratefully, pulling it down across her bare legs. "Anything new?"

"No." She's pale. I sit down next to her, wedging her in between my body and Kat's, as much to stop my own nervous tremors as to soothe hers. I track their line of sight to the small corner kitchen, where Dr Patel is in hushed conversation with a police officer. Most people have been hustled back downstairs but a handful of us have been kept back. A glance around confirms that everyone else in the room is JB.

"What's Dr Patel said?" I whisper to Kat. We're all watching the headmistress now but, as ever, she is inscrutable.

"Not a thing," Kat replies. "I mean, not to us, anyway." She turns to look at me. "Is it a bit weird there's no ambulance here?"

"I dunno." I shrug. "I guess so. I haven't thought about it."

"Well, there was one when Morgan ... er, last year?" Kat winces as soon as the words are out of her mouth. "I'm sorry, you don't remember, do you?"

"It's fine. But no, I don't remember."

"Tay? Do you think it's weird?" Kat nudges Taylor gently but she doesn't look at us. She's away with the fairies. I shake my head.

"Leave her."

We continue to watch Dr Patel talk to the police officer. Well, I say talk, but it's clear that she's in charge of the situation. He's an old white guy, thick round the middle. Hell of a moustache. Doesn't look like he could catch many hot-footed criminals. Finally he nods and they shake hands.

Did I just imagine that flash of red and white that passed between Dr Patel and the officer? I haven't seen many fifty-pound notes in real life, but that sure looked like one. More than one, in fact.

Bribery?

"Ladies." Dr Patel turns towards us as they walk past our perch on the sofa. "You may go to bed. Thank you."

Taylor stands up, the grey throw forgotten, puddling

around her feet. "You don't need me for anything? Questions, or. . ."

Dr Patel raises a manicured hand and looks pointedly at the police officer. He clears his throat, a rasping sound that makes me feel a bit sick. "Er, no, love. I've got all I need."

"Thank you, Officer Whipsnade." Dr Patel ushers him down the spiral staircase, pausing only to turn back to us one last time. "Now, girls, I won't tell you again. There is nothing more you can do here, you need rest. Off to bed. Oh, and Miss Fox? My office, please. Tomorrow. Eight a.m. sharp."

Taylor nods once and we stand in silence, like good girls. I wonder if Kat and Taylor noticed her handing over money, too. We follow her orders, though, because that's what Jewel and Bone acolytes do.

The lights are all out in the hallway and there isn't a sound except the soft hiccupping breaths I've been taking to calm myself down. Still, I bet no one's asleep. Light seeps out from beneath each closed door and once Patel's spiky footsteps disappear, a tide of whispering fills each room, the hushed sounds of shock and grief swelling out into the hallway. A couple of muffled sobs make the darkness feel even heavier. I continue to follow my deep breathing pattern, the one the therapist in hospital taught me.

Kat snaps the main light off and we climb into bed.

"How the hell am I supposed to sleep?" Taylor says as

I wrap myself in blankets. I roll over to face her, my eyes slowly adjusting to the darkness. "I feel like I'm in some kind of horror movie. First Morgan, now Jameela. Am I bad luck? Am I?"

"Shush," I whisper. Kat jumps out of bed again and checks the door handle, twisting the key when she realizes it isn't locked. "You are not bad luck."

"What if the note Jameela got wasn't a joke?" Kat suggests as she burrows back under the covers, her voice quiet in the dark room. "What if someone really did kill them both?"

"But Morton is so safe!" Even as the words leave my mouth, I know they're not true.

"It's not so safe any more, not after this." Taylor argues, her voice thick with emotion. "And did you see Patel? I'm pretty sure she paid that copper off."

"I did."

"Yep," Kat agrees. "She wasn't particularly discreet, was she?"

"So what now?" I whisper. "Are we saying someone killed them on purpose? Or are we getting carried away?"

"It seems impossible, doesn't it," Taylor says, clearing her throat quietly, as if she's been crying. I wrap the duvet tighter around myself as a shiver travels down my spine. "I mean, I know they weren't ... well, they weren't the nicest people, but who would do that?"

"Someone who wanted to scare Jameela off, maybe,"

Kat suggests quietly. "Someone who wanted something she had?"

Taylor's voice is steel cut. "What exactly does that mean?"

"Oh, no, nothing, Tay. I didn't mean. . ."

"Didn't mean what?" she spits.

I lie still beneath my covers, not daring to breathe. I wasn't expecting an argument tonight, especially not between Kat and Taylor.

"I didn't mean anything," Kat sighs. "I'm tired, I've been travelling all day. I just meant that someone might have been jealous of Jameela being head girl and thought they could scare her off, get her to leave. It could have been anyone – Ayesha, Emily. You know how bitchy that group is. They're like Mean Girls without the sassy quotes."

"Was," I correct quietly. "How bitchy that group *was*."

Silence.

"We need to stick together," Kat whispers, "just in case. OK?"

"Yes," I answer. "Taylor?"

"You're right." Taylor's response is muffled by her pillows and I hear the creak as she lifts herself up in the bed. All I can see of her is a silvered silhouette highlighted by the slight glow creeping in from the hallway. "I just can't shake the feeling I'm bad luck."

"Come on, you're not bad luck," I reassure her as Kat makes soothing noises in agreement. "It's just . . .

really unlucky that you were there both times. There's a difference, I promise. Besides, you're kind of a hero, Tay. You tried to save both of them."

Silence. And then the tiniest whisper.

"I clearly didn't try hard enough."

Morton settles back into a routine in the days after Jameela's death. Even so, she is a noticeable absence in classes, especially because everyone is constantly talking about her.

"Can you believe there hasn't been a memorial, yet? They did one for Morgan so they should do one for her too, right?" Kat quizzes us on the way down to the main hall.

"It's only Wednesday," I say. It's an early assembly today, with breakfast served after, so I'm still rubbing bleary eyes and Taylor is a literal zombie as Kat bounces along the corridor next to us. "Maybe there'll be one this morning,"

I say through a yawn. "I guess we'll find out any minute." We pause to join the back of a line waiting to go into the hall. I catch myself searching the crowd for Cole – I haven't seen him again since Monday night – and start to shuffle forwards as the large wooden doors into the hall open. The staff are already on stage and we fall into rows automatically – juniors on the left, seniors on the right – and wait, quietly chattering, until the bell rings and Dr Patel stands up.

"I can't see a picture," Kat whispers.

We snap to attention. Dr Patel goes through the motions of any other assembly – we sing something in Latin that I know word for word but could not tell you the name of; Mr Lucas, the second master, gets up and drones on about football fixtures; and my art teacher briefly mentions an exhibition that seniors can put work forward for. I'm ashamed to admit that I daydream about toast through most of it.

"Thank you, and enjoy your day." Dr Patel ends the assembly, dismissing us. My stomach rumbles.

"Toast."

"Toast," Taylor agrees. We wait to file out, but thankfully the dining hall is straight across the corridor and the crowd melts away quickly. We find a table and dump our bags before heading in separate directions.

"Get me some juice, Tay," I call after her retreating form as she heads over to the cereal bar. It looks like I'm on toast duty. Again. I head over to the big toaster by the doors and grab a pair of silver tongs. I select a slice of bread and drop it on to a little wire conveyor belt, which, moving at a glacial pace, toasts the bread. I add five more slices, ignoring the huff of a junior behind me – they'll learn. If you have the toaster, you have the toaster. I didn't make the rules.

The first slice drops and slides to the bottom, perfectly crisp and golden brown. I reach for a plate and something outside of the open doors catches my eye.

"I can't believe you won't talk to me about this." It's Frank from JB. His face is drawn and his lips are pulled back from his teeth in a snarl. I momentarily forget about the toast and watch.

"I am not doing this here, OK?" The girl in the hallway with him has her back to me; all I can see is dark, shining hair that spills down her back. "Take it to Patel, she'll know what to do."

The figure turns and I see it's Emily, Jameela's friend. Her features are carved into an angry mask as she marches into the dining hall and grabs Ayesha, who is sitting near the door with a group of JB lads.

"Are you done now? Er, hello? I said, are you finished?"

I blink and notice the impatient junior, still waiting. I look down to see I have jammed the toaster.

"Oh, yeah, sorry." I stack the toast on the plate and quickly grab a handful of butter and jam portions. The junior tuts again, but I ignore her.

The whole hall has fallen silent.

"You will talk to me now! Don't you care that your friend is dead?" Frank has followed Emily to her seat and now stands over her, glaring down. She stares back at him defiantly as spit bubbles at the corner of his mouth.

"Frank's lost it," Taylor whispers in my ear, appearing from nowhere. She hands me a tiny glass of juice and takes a piece of toast from the top of the stack. We stand, rooted to the spot as Emily jumps up and pushes Frank, both of her hands flat on his chest. He's tall, but skinny and light and he flies back to the doorway, smashing into a junior with a bowl full of cereal. Emily is obviously stronger than she looks.

"How dare you tell me I don't care?" Emily screams at him, tears streaming down her face. "She was my best friend! Not yours. I don't know why you're getting involved!"

"Because it's so obvious!" He gets to his feet, milk dripping from his blazer, and points a shaking hand at Ayesha and her table. "You're telling me that none of you have figured it out? After that note on Monday? And what about you?" He spins to point at me and Taylor, who almost chokes on her dry toast. "You two haven't realized it was a real threat, either? That Jameela was murdered? Call yourself Jewel and B..."

"MR KOWALSKI."

The entire dining hall turns to face the doors, where Dr Patel stands, her expression furious.

56

"She looks like she's going to kill him," Taylor whispers. I can't help but agree. Dr Patel's usually calm exterior is ruffled, betrayed by slightly bulging eyes and pursed lips. There's a red flush to her cheeks that clashes with the forest-green silk shirt she's wearing.

"My office. Now." She doesn't wait for him, instead spinning on a stiletto heel. Her footsteps ring down the corridor. Frank follows, his shoulders slumped now, the fight gone out of him.

"That's the last we'll see of him," Kat bellows as she joins us. The volume level in the room has gone from zero all the way up to ten in a matter of seconds, and my ears ring as we sit back at our table. "He's done for. Reckon she'll suspend him?"

"I really don't know. Have you ever seen Patel so angry?" Taylor asks as she takes another slice from the plate I forgot I was holding. I put it in the middle along with the jam and butter.

"No, never," I reply. I crane my neck around to see Emily, who is still in floods of tears, being comforted by Ayesha while the boys look on awkwardly. A cleaning supervisor is sorting out the mess left on the floor. When I look back at the plate, there's only one slice of toast left.

"And it's cold," I say.

Kat smiles apologetically. "Sorry, I was hungry. Here." She throws a banana at me and I pull a face. I grab the last slice of toast and smear it with peanut butter, slicing the banana into little coins that I place in a neat pattern on top. I eat lost in thought, chewing slowly. Frank knows the rules. We never speak about Jewel and Bone – and certainly not in a crowded dining hall. What on earth did he know that would have caused him to lose control like that?

11

"Liz? Lizzie? Rise and shine, sleepyhead." I force my eyes
open to find Kat's face looming over mine and sit up so
fast I almost headbutt her. "Whoa, sorry! Your alarm was
going off, that's all. Were you taking a nap?"

I try my best to refocus but my head is fuzzy. "Water?"

"Here." Kat thrusts a cold bottle into my hand and I
gulp it down gratefully. "Better?"

"Yeah, thanks." Bed. Wednesday. Morton. I kick the
twisted duvet from my legs and push myself up to sitting,
rearranging the pillows behind my back. "I thought naps
made you feel better. I feel worse than I did before."

"Ah, you need practice, that's all. Naps are the best."

Kat joins me on the end of my bed, making a pile of the books and notepads that have surrounded me as I slept. I never, ever nap. I'm usually lucky to fall asleep at all. Kat places my stuff on the floor, kicks off her trainers and sits back, cross-legged.

My twin bed is in the corner of our room, pushed up against the wall so you can use it like a sofa. I put the water bottle on to my bedside table, a squat, wooden thing with a lockable drawer and cabinet underneath, and lean my head back, looking up at the lone window.

"What time is it?"

"Seven thirty. Good job we don't have too much prep this week; you won't get away with sleeping all afternoon this year. You did miss dinner, though."

"Please tell me you sneaked me something?"

Kat grins and produces a little paper bag. "Not exactly gourmet, but the best I could get away with."

"Thanks." I take the bag from her and pull out an apple, a squished bread roll and a little pat of butter. That will do. "So," I say, ripping the paper bag apart and setting my meagre dinner out on it, "what did I miss?"

"Not much. People still talking about Frank's outburst. He's all sheepish; Patel must've given him a massive rollicking this morning. No news on another JB meeting, though, so I guess we'll have to wait until the usual one on Monday. Everyone's on edge. The common rooms open on Saturday – we get lunch there this year. Oh, and your hot new friend is eating with the science kids but Marcus is trying to lure him to the dark side."

I laugh as I tear the bread roll open and paint it with butter, using the foil wrapper to spread it. "He's hardly my friend; I only spoke to him on Monday night." I take a bite and relish the salt. I didn't know real butter was a thing until I got to Morton. "What else?"

"Patel came in to speak to us all, which was weird. I don't think I've ever seen her in the dining hall apart from this morning. She started to talk about Open Evening – it's next Thursday, by the way – and then she finally acknowledged Jameela after, what, two whole days? Said her parents had requested a private ceremony, it was a tragedy, blah, blah, blah, no further action being taken but we can go for counselling if we *really* want to."

"Oh, please, as if we have time for therapy. I literally fell asleep under a pile of books this afternoon. So that's it? Nothing's being looked into?"

"That's it. It's one hundred per cent dodgy, though."

We are interrupted by a voice coming from the doorway. "Haven't you forgotten something?" Taylor flips her hair, sending a silky curtain over her shoulder so I can see a shiny, black shield pinned to her lapel.

I sit up straight. "No. Kat would have said!"

"I wanted the girl herself to tell you," Kat grins. "Go on then, Fox."

"Oh, if I must." Taylor clears her throat and beams at

me. "I was officially announced as head girl. Patel told me yesterday morning after, well, you know, and I wasn't allowed to say anything until now."

"Taylor! I can't believe I slept through the whole thing!"

"You'll be there on Monday, when I'm sworn in. That's when it matters. Anyway, guess who's the new deputy?"

"No, not *Emily*." I groan.

"Yep. She beat me to that robe by a millisecond on initiation night, didn't she?" Kat shrugs, though I can tell she's upset. I reach over to pat her knee.

"She's going to be so. . ." I start, but Taylor cuts me off. "Insufferable?"

"I was going to say mean, but insufferable works. I'm sorry, Kat. If you hadn't hung back for me that day, you would have got in there before her."

"Hey, don't be. My parents will send me to university anyway, even if it means racking up a lifetime's worth of debt." She shrugs. "Emily might not have that."

"Now who's the nice one?" I grin, pulling a cushion from behind me to throw in her direction.

"Well." Taylor glances down at her lapel, as though she can't believe her luck. "Let's hope this badge isn't cursed, or something."

"Third time lucky?" Kat suggests.

"Nice, Kat." Taylor laughs despite herself as she looks around our cosy dorm room. "I guess I'm moving out, then."

"Not until we pick your university with you!" Kat leaps

62

from the bed and twirls her around, Taylor laughing and spinning like the little plastic doll in a music box.

"Oh, don't you worry." Taylor collapses backwards on to her bed, her hair and arms splayed out above her. "I did that weeks ago."

The rest of the week passed pretty quietly. Well, as quietly as it could when there were whispers of murder and conspiracy in the air. I've only seen Frank once, in classics, and he looked pale, withdrawn. I don't think anyone has spoken to him; they're scared of getting into trouble by association.

"Are you sure we won't get caught?" It's Friday evening and yet again I seem to be watching Taylor debate over an outfit in the mirror, only this time I'm draped upside down over an armchair in the senior lounge. My head is hanging down over the seat, the ends of my hair just tickling the floor. I'm starting to get pins and needles and my eyes go fuzzy as she traipses to the doorway of her new room. I'm so tired I could sleep like this, but I promised I'd go to the woods with her – another senior rite of passage for the first week back.

"I don't really care, Lizzie. I just need to *feel* something." I flip myself upright, enjoying the feeling of the blood draining back into my limbs, tingles dissipating. "How's this?"

"Perfect, as usual." Her vermillion locks are piled on

her head in a huge, messy topknot, tendrils pulled out to frame her face. A pair of tightly belted mom jeans and an off-the-shoulder knitted cream cardigan – that has only been slightly buttoned up – over a lacy crop top complete the look.

"You're sure?"

"Yes, perfectly preppy-casual-gorgeous." I look down at my battered joggers. "Suppose I better get changed, then."

Taylor holds out her hands and I let her grasp mine and pull me from the chair. "Er, yeah. I can't let you talk to Cole in your scruffs."

"Cole is coming?" Hmm, this is starting to almost seem like a good idea.

"Yes, Cole is coming. He's pretty cool." She gives me a sly, sideways glance as she drags me through into the head girl's bedroom. "Like you haven't noticed."

The corners of my mouth twitch. "Oh, maybe just a little bit. . ."

"Well, you need to borrow something." She starts to burrow through the mountain of clothes on her bed. "God, I love having the space to be messy – oh here." She holds out a scrap of fabric and immediately drops it at the look on my face. "Yeah, you're right. Oh! Here – this one will be perfect!"

I take the thin woollen jumper dress from her and hold it up to me in the mirror. "Do you think I can carry this off?"

"Of course you can! Look." She stretches the material across my shoulders. "The boat neck flatters your hot new bob and it's a bit fancy but still slouchy and casual. Wear it with your Converse and you'll be effortless."

"Hmmm." I pull my T-shirt off and slide into the dress, shuffling my joggers off simultaneously. It's one of those dresses that clings in all the right places but skims over the other bits. The long sleeves are slim, trailing down to a flared cuff, and tiny black metallic stars are stitched all over, catching the light but otherwise invisible. Taylor was right – the neckline makes my hair look vaguely presentable, though I miss the curtain of blonde I used to hide behind.

"You look gorgeous." She grins, holding up a huge eyeshadow palette in the reflection behind me. "But I am totally going to do your make-up."

"No, I. . ."

"Did I mention Cole?"

I sigh and take a seat on the edge of the bed.

"Fine," I say. "Do your worst."

12

Sneaking out of the main building at Morton is ridiculously easy. It's almost like they trust us – either that or they don't care at all. We walk out of the back door in the dining hall and make a run for the bushes behind the huge dumpsters out there. It's another place that I have yet to explore and I feel a little bubble of anticipation at the thought of a proper party. One that involves Cole.

It's later than I thought, going on for eight thirty, and the sky is all pink and dusky and gorgeous. Kat is waiting for us in the thicket of trees behind the dining hall, a couple of other acolytes in tow. She jumps up and bounces over to us immediately – that girl has way too

66

much energy – and we all exchange greetings, waving and tapping over our hearts.

"God, we've been here for ever. What took so long?" she bellows. Then Taylor drags me forward and Kat lets out a wolf whistle.

"You can't rush a masterpiece," Taylor brags. I mean, she did do a good job, I admit. I have that dewy no-make-up-I-woke-up-like-this vibe going on and she tonged a couple of messy curls into my hair so I have what she called a "sexy bedhead", which is not something I think exists in real life. She curled my hair with her straighteners, which I have no idea how to do, and it has brought out natural highlights I wasn't aware I had. She's got such a good eye for this stuff. I'm never confident enough to try anything different. But tonight, I very much look as though my naturally glowing self just threw any old thing on – and yet I look fantastic.

I love it.

"Liz, you hottie!" Kat smiles at me appraisingly and raises an eyebrow in that way everyone wishes they could do. She looks back at Taylor. "Cole?"

Taylor nods. "Cole."

"Right, that's enough thanks," I say and aim for the others. "Come on, let's get out of here before we get caught."

"Deal." Kat runs back to the other girls, Beck, a willowy blonde who's in JB but is definitely one of the quieter members, and Caroline, who is indeed wearing her favourite V-necked crop top. Kat wiggles her eyebrows at me when she sees that I've noticed and I try to stifle a laugh as we follow them, Taylor's bag clanking as we go.

It's a lot darker in here than I thought and I think longingly of the torch on my iPhone, but it's locked up in Dr Patel's office with everyone else's – part of the contract when you sign up for Morton. That plus no social media *and* monitored internet time that you have to pre-book on weekends only. Safeguarding – something the school prides itself on.

We crunch through the dry forest floor. The grounds around Morton are ridiculous, like acres and acres of forest and fields. If you were out here on your own and something happened, it could be days before you were found. . .

"Liz? Helllooooo?" I snap back to the present. Taylor is peering at me, her brow slightly furrowed. "You OK? We lost you for a minute then."

"Yeah, sorry." I gesture to my head. "Just, you know. I'm fine, though, honest."

"Okaaaay." She draws out the word, as though she thinks it's anything but OK. "If you say so. Look." She points to where the trees are starting to clear a bit and I see a warm yellow flicker. "The boys have started a fire."

"Of course they have." Kat snorts. "So macho."

"Some of us like macho." Taylor smirks, as Marcus's

tall, broad frame comes into view. "See you girls later."

I wander around the little enclosure, observing the scene like a mountaineer who's just conquered Everest. I dreamed of evenings like these over the summer, from my horrible single bed in our horrible little flat. I was stuck in that room, listening to my parents and their shady friends drinking and who knows what else in the living room. Every time I snuck out to use the loo, some loser would eye me up and down like I was a piece of meat. My parents didn't notice. I have to pinch myself now my life is like something out of a TV series about glossy teens whose parents are never around.

But it's real. It's mine. This is life at Morton, especially when you're part of Jewel and Bone. This year is going to be full of chances to go to parties I've never dreamed of, to meet people of real influence and power – people who can help me leave my old life behind. I just need one donor to see my potential, to sponsor my education. At university, that's when it will really begin. This is just a warm-up.

I wave shyly at faces I recognize and a couple I don't, not particularly well, anyway. All the other acolytes are here, but many of the other seniors are, too. Logs have been dragged around a small fire to make seats and a few kids have spread blankets on grass that's scattered with the occasional golden leaf. We're right in the middle of those perfect ember days of summer, the turning weather clinging on to memories of warmth.

"Hey." A voice greets me and I turn to face Cole, my breath catching as I remember exactly how gorgeous he is.

"Hey," I echo, somewhat stupidly.

"You sitting down?" He points to an empty log on the far side of the fire. It will fit us both if we sit kind of close. Um, yes, I'm sitting down.

"Sure," I say instead, stretching my face into what I hope is a confident smile, and my feet crunch on tiny twigs underfoot as we head towards it. He gestures for me to sit first and, sure enough, there's only a whisper of air between us when we are both settled.

"Sorry," he says. "Kinda cosy, isn't it. Here." He slides off the log on to the ground. Still close, but I'm grateful for the breathing space. "Better?"

"Yeah, thanks."

We sit in silence for a moment, watching the flames catch on the kindling, small, sharp cracks piercing the quiet shadows. Cole leans forwards to poke it with a stick he's found on the floor before throwing it on to the fire.

"Dunno why I did that," he says, slightly sheepish. "There's just something about a fire, isn't there? It's hypnotic."

"I know what you mean." The flames *are* mesmerizing: the way the fire eats away at anything in its path, doing whatever it needs to fulfil its purpose in life.

"Most serial killers begin as arsonists, you know." Kat's voice interrupts and I refocus as she hovers over us with a drinks cooler. "Beer?"

"Thanks." Cole reaches for one and I find myself studying his long, elegant hands again. "Liz? Oh wait, you don't. . ."

"It's fine." I smile as Kat hands me a Diet Coke. "Kat's got me covered."

"Of course. Here." She pulls a drink out for herself and waves a hand at Cole. "Scootch," she says.

He grins apologetically and retakes the seat next to me so Kat can flop into his place, though this time I feel the top of his leg press against mine. I tap my nails against the aluminium can and then pop the tab and take a huge swig to cover my grin, immediately regretting it as the bubbles threaten to make a reappearance.

Thankfully, Cole doesn't notice. "What did you mean? About serial killers being arsonists?"

I start to laugh and cut Kat off before she can get started. "Ignore her. Kat's doing psychology – *everything* is the trait of a serial killer."

"Not everything," she argues, grinning at me, "just, you know, the triad." She places her bottle on the ground between her crossed legs and starts ticking off things on her fingers. "One, arson. Serial killers generally liked setting fires as kids. Second, wetting the bed."

"Wait." Cole looks uncomfortable. "Wetting the bed means you want to kill people?"

"Why?" Kat eyes him and takes a swig from her drink, replacing the bottle slowly. "You worried?"

"No, I er." Cole takes a drink too and I smother a giggle.

"Kat." I nudge her with my foot. "Play nice."

"I am! No, it doesn't, but with some other traits it's a definite red flag."

"Right." He looks relieved and I have to hide another giggle. "So what's the last one? You said triad, that's three, right?"

"Right, so you have arson, bed-wetting and the last one" – she lowers her voice, the sockets of her eyes hollow in the gloom – "which is where it gets really dark, is animal torture."

"Kat, you're not telling the new boy about serial killers, are you?" Taylor's voice sounds from behind me and I lean my head back to face her. She grins down at me, Marcus's arm wrapped around her waist.

"Oh, she is," I say. "We're on to animal torture already."

"Kat!" Taylor admonishes her, as Cole looks around in bewilderment.

"Is this normal?" he asks me under his breath, as Kat and Taylor rib one another over our heads.

"Afraid so," I laugh, but Kat interrupts.

"Only when I'm vetting potential boy—"

"Er, thanks, Kat." I kick her a little harder this time and feel Cole's eyes burning into me.

"Come on, you weirdo." Taylor ruffles my hair gently as she takes Kat's arm. "Leave these two alone. I'll even let you tell me your Zodiac killer theory again."

"Well, how can I resist an offer like that?" Kat climbs to her feet, brushing bits of forest floor off her toned legs. "Later, lovebirds," she trills, skipping over to the other side of the clearing. I immediately put my head in my hands.

"Oh my God, I am so sorry," I mutter from between my fingers. "She's just a bit full on, you know?"

"Hey, I get it. She's your friend, she's looking out for you. I'd probably do the same if I was her and some new guy came in and started talking to the prettiest girl at school."

My hands are glued to my face. *Prettiest girl?* Did he just call me the prettiest girl at school?

"You look nice, tonight, by the way," he continues.

Liz, take your face out of your hands. Slowly, that's it. Good, now look at him.

I look at him.

He's smiling at me.

"I like your hair like that." I realize he's trying to fill the silence because I am acting like a total weirdo, so I go to my default setting of self-deprecation.

"Thanks, it used to be long, though. I hate it like this."

"It did? Why did you cut it if you don't like it?"

I shrug. "No choice. I had an ... accident last year." I part the waves a bit to show him the tufty bits. "I hit my head. Had to have some pretty gnarly stitches."

"I'm so sorry, I didn't realize. How are you now?"

"Oh, fine." I wave the question off, like I always do.

"Apparently I could get seizures or something, but I've been OK so far." I hold up the cola. "But that's why I don't drink."

"Well." Cole holds up his beer and clinks it against my can. "I'm glad you're doing well." He takes a sip and smiles at me. "And, for the record, I like the hair."

It turns out that it's easy talking to Cole — easier than talking to anyone, even Taylor and Kat. It's like a clamp in my chest has released a little, and I realize it's relief. So I keep going, telling him about my miserable time over the holidays, a summer of painkillers and wasted days watching the sky from a dirty window. I leave out some details, of course. It's hard to discuss things without giving away JB, sometimes.

"Jeez." He opens a second beer. "That must've been a lot to deal with. I'm sorry."

"Thanks." I feel I should be honest, so I say, "We weren't friends exactly, but" — I gesture round the clearing —

"Morton's pretty small. You can't help but get to know each other."

"In that case, fill me in. Give me a rundown of everyone here." He leans back and gestures around at the others in the clearing. I'm grateful for the change of topic and scan the crowd.

"Well, you kind of know Marcus and Taylor. King and Queen of Morton." I smile. "You've met Kat, she scared you – pretty standard... Oh, here we go." I point to a tall, slim white boy with a shock of dark hair. "That's Frank."

"Oh, yeah. He's the dude who was shouting about Jameela in the dining hall, right?"

"Right." I wince. "That was pretty bad. He's in my classics class. I always thought he was really quiet but obviously not. He's here for English as his first subject. Some kind of writing scholar – Kat says his stuff is amazing but it's super dark. He can be very... intense, I guess. Oh, and he has these really striking blue eyes, but whatever you do, don't mention it to him or you'll never hear the end of it. He loves to talk about them." Cole snorts as I scan the crowd, my eyes landing on a short girl with sad eyes. "That's Emily, I dunno if you remember her from the pyjama party?"

"She was Jameela's friend. The one Frank was yelling at."

"Yeah. She and Jameela were both besties with Morgan last year; there were four of them in this clique – Morgan,

Jameela, Emily and Ayesha. I know you're not meant to speak ill of the dead, but they were kind of the mean girls of the junior class."

"She doesn't look mean," Cole observes. I take in Emily's hunched frame and vacant stare. No, she doesn't look mean.

"I guess losing friends changes you," I say. "Emily's here for maths, like Jameela was; she does classics with me too, though. Can't remember what her other subject is. She used to do this trick last year, where you fired massive numbers at her and she'd just multiply them straight off, do it in her head. I don't think she ever got one wrong."

"That's a pretty cool party trick. You got one?" He's smiling.

"Of course." I go to flick my hair before remembering it's gone. Ugh. "I can recite all the kings and queens of England since William the Conqueror. In order. With the dates they ruled."

"Serious?"

"Of course. What about you?"

"Periodic table. I can tell you the order and letters for every element. Could probably do it backwards too, never tried, though." He looks stricken for a moment. "I've just realized that makes me a huge geek, doesn't it?"

"Welcome to the club." I smile, gesturing around. "We are literally the biggest geeks in the country. It's wonderful."

Cole beams at me. "Agreed. Carry on. Who's next?"

"Er, let's see." I nod my head towards the girl Emily is with. "That's Ayesha, the final of the foursome." She's subdued too, sitting close to Emily and Frank. Presumably they've made up after what happened on Wednesday. She's nervously fiddling with her gauzy blue headscarf, undoing and retying it over and over again as they speak in hushed tones. I wonder if they are still dwelling on the note. "Fluent in about five languages but zero common sense."

"Hey, there's nothing wrong with that." Cole nudges me gently. "We're not all blessed with practicality, you know."

"Oh, no, really?" I tease, turning to catch his eye. "Then I'm afraid we can't be friends."

"Don't say that." Cole brushes his hand on the side of my leg and I hold in a little hiccup of breath, forcing myself to focus on the others while simultaneously letting my hand drift to my lap and rest next to his. I have to clear my throat before I can carry on.

"Those two are Joe and Ethan." I point to a short, stocky boy with tight black curls and a skinny kid with cut-glass cheekbones and skin even paler than mine. "They're both here for computer science. Ethan was Morgan's boyfriend. . ." I trail off, realizing every single person I've mentioned is a Jewel and Bone acolyte.

Which means that every one of them is a potential suspect — at least according to Frank.

"What about those two?" Cole points over to where Kat is now holding court in the clearing, minus her T-shirt, taking shots out of two people's bellybuttons.

"Oh, God." I groan, but I can't help laughing. "That's Beck and Caroline. They do English with Kat and are, er, easily influenced." Cole's eyes are wide as they resume their seats on the floor with three boys from the languages department, cross-legged, each holding a fanned-out hand of cards. Caroline's lipstick is smudged and her crop top is askew. One of the boys, Luke, another acolyte, is pulling a tight black T-shirt over his head, a finely carved set of abs peeking through. "Strip/Dare Poker. Kat made it up last year – strip poker meets truth or dare. I can't tell you *how* many items of clothing she has lost this way."

Cole laughs before peeling his eyes away and I feel the tiniest little tug of jealousy under my ribs. "Good to know that even us geeks know how to have fun, I guess. Though I don't know if I'm ready for that much fun." He lowers his voice. "Your friend Kat kind of scares me."

"Yeah," I agree, "she scares most people. She's the best, though. These are the things that happen when you can't get on the internet, I guess." I sit up straight, realizing I've been doing most of the talking. "What about you? Glad to be here, at Morton?"

"Hell, yeah. I was lucky to get in. It was like a dream, you know? Like winning the lottery or something."

"I know what you mean. How did your parents take it?"

"They were chuffed." He smiles. "Mum's from Taiwan and always dreamed her son would get a top-notch education – she never did. I had a scholarship at the local grammar school. I thought she was proud then, but when my year tutor called us in over the summer to meet Dr Patel and she offered me a place here, I thought Mum was going to have a heart attack. She practically packed my bags that night." He smiles at the memory and I find myself obsessing over a teeny freckle on his cheek. "I hadn't even heard of it before then – but I feel very lucky. Anyway, what about you?" He sips at his beer. "Were your parents the same? I mean you got in here last year, you must be super clever. Not like us waiting list dweebs. I bet they were proud."

"Yeah." I think of the day I sat in my headteacher's office with Dr Patel. Dad had stayed in bed and Mum was pacing up and down outside, one of her so-called friend's dramas playing down the phone she held in one hand, taking long puffs of a cigarette with the other. We watched her from the window and I realized she wasn't even slightly aware that she was late for our meeting.

"Yeah," I repeat. "They were chuffed, too. Anyway!" I force brightness into my voice. "How's your first week been? Is science here everything you dreamed it would be?"

"Absolutely. The equipment in the lab is insane, like university-standard. There are machines worth at least quarter of a mil. It's like I've died and come to geek heaven." He winces. "Sorry, poor choice of words given ... everything. You know what I mean, though, right?"

"Of course I do." I reassure him. "I thought about this place all summer. I couldn't wait to get back. Has Marcus been looking after you?"

"Yeah, he's pretty chill, seems like a good guy. Taylor's been great, too. You guys are tight, right?"

"She's my best friend. Not sure what I'd do without her."

"That's nice." He slips me a glance from beneath his brow. "Everyone needs someone they feel like that about."

My cheeks flame again and I take a sip of my drink, realize it's empty and style it out the best I can.

"Yeah." I force myself to catch his eye and let a shy smile stretch my lips as his warm fingers start to close around my cool ones. "Yeah, they do."

"Er, sorry to interrupt." I tear my eyes away from Cole's and look up to see Frank standing there. The fire is smouldering behind him and Emily and Ayesha are throwing fistfuls of dirt on the dying cinders. "The juniors have called to say Patel's on the rampage. We need to get back to the dorms ASAP."

"Great," I mutter, watching his retreating form. I get to my feet and look around for anything that might have been left behind – mainly items of Kat's clothing.

"What does that mean?" Cole says.

"It means that we are going to be in big trouble if we don't get out of here, now."

I always forget how quickly night can fall, even when you're expecting it. Everyone has scattered and the woods seem huge and empty.

Eerie.

"Hey," Cole whispers from behind me, "how did someone call Frank to tell him Patel was coming? I thought we weren't allowed phones. Oh, and his eyes are really blue, aren't they? He totally wears contacts."

"Oh, sweet summer child." I smile, hoping he gets the *GoT* reference. "We all have these." I pause and lean down to pull a tiny phone from the collar of my high tops, where it fits snugly behind my ankle bone. "There's always a couple of first years on Dr Patel watch. They keep a look out and ring whoever the designated senior is when there's a party going on. It's weird, we have nothing much to do with them apart from that, but it's like a tradition – I think Morgan and Jameela did it last year when we were the juniors. Frank must have been the designated senior tonight."

"But burner phones, Cersei?" I knew he'd get it. "Seriously?"

"Yep." I tuck it back down and start walking again, weaving beneath the trees and keeping my eyes open for a flash of light that might indicate someone looking for us. "They're old Nokias – you can only text and call on them but the battery lasts for ever. And they have this properly addictive snake game on them, too." I pause, a twig snapping somewhere up ahead. "Wait there," I whisper to Cole. I sneak forward and hear it again. "Quiet, I think there's someone there," I hiss, turning back to him. "We need to go back."

But I'm alone.

"Cole?" I try, a little louder. I squint through the darkness and feel the scar along my head start to itch, the way it does when anxiety makes my skin prickle. "Cole?"

Nothing.

I stand still and shut my eyes, listening carefully. I'm not sure how much time passes but finally I hear another crunch underfoot and my eyes fly open, searching the gloom in the direction of the sound.

"Cole?"

My voice sounds small but too loud at the same time, echoing through the inky dark. I will my feet forwards and start to walk, panting as though I've just run laps. Sweat trickles down the nape of my neck and I realize I'm terrified.

Of what?

It's funny, isn't it, how your body knows when something's not right. My feet don't want to walk this way and my adrenaline is pumping so hard I feel sick. There's such a sudden sense of wrongness in the air, it's almost tangible. I can feel it.

"Cole?"

"Liz." A voice croaks in response this time and I speed up at the sound of it, rounding a tight knot of trees in the dark. I fumble for my tiny phone, knowing the light will be pathetic but it will be something, so when I stumble on the scene I only see sepia-toned snatches of it. "He . . . I think he's. . ."

He doesn't finish his sentence, but I see it all. Cole, kneeling in the leaves. The sticky, viscous red on a jagged rock.

A pale, dead hand, curled around a plastic inhaler.

14

I did not set out with murderous intentions tonight but that boy caught me by surprise. I should have expected it, after his outburst earlier this week. I should have known that someone would be watching. I mean, that's what I do. I should have seen it coming.

It was his own fault. He didn't have to get involved, I thought he had been scared off. He wasn't part of the original plan. Cornering me like that in the woods, shoving the inhaler under my nose. Said he knew I'd poisoned it, he'd figured it out. Please. As if he could have known what I was planning. He probably ended the party early on purpose, so he could try and get me on my own in the dark. Intimidate me.

Well, that didn't work out too well for him, did it?

He didn't let go of the damn inhaler, though. I'll need to figure out how to get that back at some point, just in case it can be traced to me.

Yes — it was his fault. He should have left it alone. The rock I found in my hand was just right. Heavier than I thought it would be, but not too heavy.

No, it was the perfect weight to smash his meddling little head in.

15

"Cole?" My eyes dart between the bloody rock and Frank's limp body. He's face down and I move the light away from the matted mess that was his head so I don't have to look at it any more. "What happened?"

"I was going to ask you the same thing. I just . . . found him." He chokes the words out, his features bone-white in the gloom. "I tripped over this." He holds the rock out, away from him, searching for somewhere to put it down.

"OK, let's put that down. It's OK." I start to edge over to him, around the body, when I stop.

I don't know him. How can I trust him?

"Liz, I didn't. . . Oh God, please don't think. . ." He

breaks off as he retches, bringing up the contents of his stomach on the forest floor. I kneel down next to him.

"Hey, shush, it's OK. Here, give me that." I prise the rock from his hand gingerly. I can just about make out blood and hair on it, try not to get my fingers in it. My own dinner threatens to make a reappearance.

"Lizzie?" A familiar voice hisses through the darkness and a figure emerges. "What are you . . . OH MY GOD! Is that . . . Frank?" Kat's voice shoots up several octaves and I jump up, pulling her down to floor level, though I don't know who – or what – we're hiding from.

"We just found him and—"

"Lizzie." Kat's voice is calm and measured, which is how I know she's freaking out. "You're holding a really big rock. With lots of blood on it." I look down at my hand and the rock falls from my fingers in slow motion. Kat continues to talk but my ears are muffled, like someone had stuck wedges of cotton wool into them, or I'm underwater. I hear her say, "Is he alive?"

"What?" Cole's head snaps up.

"Frank, is he alive?"

It never even occurred to me. Between the rock and the bloody mess of his head, I just assumed he wasn't. Kat goes into full crisis mode, snapping orders at Cole to help her roll Frank on to his side so she can check his pulse.

Nothing.

"I'm going to start CPR," Kat says, rolling him

unceremoniously on to his back, the pink inhaler bouncing away from his hand. I wince as his body thuds back to the ground, little eddies of dry soil dancing around him.

"I'm not sure if that's a good idea, Ms Paphitis." My head snaps up as the figure of Dr Patel emerges from the trees with the groundskeeper, trailing behind her. "We can take over from here."

"But he might be alive," she says, her voice small as she follows the beam of light from the groundskeeper's torch to Frank's lifeless eyes.

She drops him as though his cold, dead skin has burnt her fingers.

Dr Patel waves the groundskeeper forwards and he begins to cover the body – Frank – with a dark plastic sheet.

"I need to know what happened here tonight. But first, go back to the school."

The headmistress ushers us away and I climb to my feet slowly, my eyes on a faint pink gleam in the grass. Jameela's inhaler.

I don't know what makes me do it, but I inch my hand over and pick it up, sliding it into my long, flared sleeve as I stand.

"Listen very carefully. I want you three to go back to the main building." Dr Patel looks at Cole and takes in the dark stain on his T-shirt. "Straight to my office, do you understand? Don't speak to anyone or stop to clean up. I will radio Nurse Templeton to meet you there and we will take care of" – she waves a hand vaguely behind her – "this. I will be along very shortly. Do I make myself clear?"

"Yes, Dr Patel," we mutter. Is it weird that this seems . . . normal? Is this what shock feels like?

We shuffle along in silence, not bothering to sneak back in but walking right in the front doors of the school. The brightly lit hallways smell of citrus and beeswax and the usually soft lights pluck at my eyes. I notice that Kat's top is inside out.

I think I'm getting a migraine.

"Come on," I say to Cole. His face is ashen and there is a smear of blood on his cheek, where he has tried to wipe away the dirt and tears. Now all three decorate his face like some kind of macabre warpaint. "The office is this way."

The school is silent. It must be after ten now and lights out is at half past, so anyone with any sense is in bed.

When did I start shaking so hard?

We stop outside of the door, a huge, wooden slab with a shining plaque on it. *Dr Patel, Headmistress.*

"Do you think we should go in?" Kat whispers. Her hand is shaking too as it reaches for the polished brass handle. "Did she say wait inside?"

"I can't remember." My teeth are chattering now and I'm freezing, trembling in my borrowed dress. "Cole?"

He stares blankly at the wall.

"Let's just go in," Kat decides. The handle turns easily and the door swings inwards with no sound. Patel's office is fairly stark, no family photos or anything personal. There are some certificates on the wall behind her desk, which is carved from another monstrous piece of wood. Three low-slung armchairs line this side and we stumble towards them. A tall, wing-backed chair stands sentry on the opposite side, waiting for Dr Patel to come back.

"Do you want some water?" Kat asks. I sink into one of the green leather guest chairs as Kat helps herself to a drink. I shake my head but she fills two more paper cups and brings them over for me and Cole anyway. I take mine gratefully but forget all about the inhaler wedged into my sleeve. It falls out, bouncing off the floor.

"What's this?" She grabs it with her too-fast reflexes.

"Frank was holding it." Cole's voice is quiet, his eyes firmly on the lip of his paper cup. "When I found him."

Kat sinks into an empty seat and studies the little pink inhaler. A faint red lipstick mark still decorates the mouthpiece and she turns it over and over in her hands as I watch, mesmerized.

"What was Frank doing with Jameela's inhaler?" she mumbles, more to herself than either of us.

"I don't know," I say. My voice cracks. "It doesn't make any sense."

I switch my gaze between her and the white institutional clock on the wall. Where do you even buy those? I'm sure every school and hospital has the same ones. I saw loads this summer.

"Ah, you're here. Thank you." We all jump at Dr Patel's voice – those hinges really are well oiled. Kat slides the inhaler under her leg as Dr Patel strides to her chair and sits down. Her camel-coloured blazer is immaculate, even though she's just been dealing with a dead body in the woods, and she's not the slightest bit out of breath. "Now." She folds her fingers into one another and places her hands on the desk. "Tell me what happened."

We all stare at her for a second. She gives a little sigh. "Cole, please."

"I don't know." He looks like he's about to cry. "We were walking and—"

"Walking where?"

Cole shrugs miserably and Dr Patel switches her gaze to me. "Elizabeth?"

Full name. Yikes. I let out a long breath.

"We were at a senior party," I admit, feeling Kat's eyes boring into me. The nicest girl at Morton strikes again. "It was just a few of us in the woods. We were on our way back when – well, when we got split up in the woods and..." I trail off, fully aware of how pathetic this sounds.

"And?"

"I found Frank," Cole admits. "I was looking for Liz and then I tripped on a rock and fell. I picked it up and then

I saw ... him. And his head was all..." He stops, patting the back of his own head and wincing.

"You didn't touch the body?"

"No. Well, except when Kat came. She wanted to see if he was still alive." Kat nods in agreement.

Dr Patel's gaze flicks to me. "Where were you while this was going on, Elizabeth?"

"With Cole, well mostly. I got turned all around in the woods and lost him for a little while. When I finally found him, he was with the ... with Frank."

"And Frank was already dead?"

I nod. The image of Cole holding the bloody rock flashes before my eyes.

Dr Patel nods. "All right. Well, that's quite enough for tonight. Get some rest. This is a police matter now."

"Like Jameela?" Kat mutters.

"Excuse me?" Dr Patel's voice could freeze the water in my cup.

"Nothing, sorry, Dr Patel."

"Indeed." A knock on the door saves Kat from whatever Dr Patel is about to say next. "Yes?"

"You asked for me?"

"Come in, Nurse." The door swings open as Nurse Templeton, a short, matronly woman, steps into the office. A green first-aid kit dangles from her hand. "My apologies, I don't think we need you after all, we don't seem to actually have any injuries here." She looks at each of us in turn. "Do we?"

We shake our heads in silence.

"Oh." There's an edge of annoyance to Nurse Templeton's voice. I look at her closely and see the collar of her nightgown poking out from beneath her uniform. We've dragged her out of bed. "I might as well check them over, now I'm here."

"No need," Dr Patel says. The two women stare at one another until Nurse Templeton drops her gaze to the floor.

"Very well." She admits defeat, but not before glancing over us once more. "Make sure you come and see me if you need to, please."

"I'm sure they will." Dr Patel doesn't give us the chance to respond. "Goodnight."

The door clicks behind the nurse's retreating figure.

"Now." Dr Patel stands up, pushing back the large chair and pointing us towards the door. I stand up in a trance and follow the others. "Take yourselves off to bed. I would rather you didn't discuss this with anyone for now, not until we find out what has happened. Chances are Frank merely tripped and fell in the dark. An unfortunate accident." Dr Patel opens the door. "Try not to worry about it too much. Goodnight."

The door shuts silently behind us as we emerge into the hall and stare at one another. There's a fire in Cole's eyes.

"An *accident*?" he hisses.

"It could be..." I try, but the words sound wrong.

Kat is looking at the inhaler in her hand.

"I think Cole's right. Listen, what if..." She pauses, looking from the inhaler to the closed door and then back to Cole. To me.

"What if what?" I press.

"What if Frank figured out Morgan and Jameela were murdered? And that's why he was killed."

16

I take my time walking down the long, curving staircase and pause for a second at the bottom, letting the sunlight that washes through the long windows warm me. I only managed to sleep for a couple of hours and I feel drained, hollowed out.

I've only just stopped shaking.

I pick up the pace again and follow the corridor over to the west wing of the house, passing through the entrance hall and past Mr Lucas, the second master's, office. Morton is quiet – it's early for a Saturday morning, just before nine. Most kids take today as a rest day and work through Sundays instead.

"Hey." Cole is leaning against the honey-coloured wall next to a huge pair of glass-panelled doors. He straightens up as I approach.

"Hey." Eloquent, Liz. "Ready for your official tour?"

Cole jams his hands deep into the pockets of his grey sweatpants. "Tour? I thought that was Taylor's job, you know, as head girl and whatever."

"I made her trade with me. She was happy to; I think she's got a lot on this year." I gesture to the shining prefect badge that I've pinned to my plain black T-shirt. "I'm authorized to do them, too." I study his face. "Disappointed?"

"No," he says softly, taking his hands out of his pockets again and tugging at the toggles of the zipper on his hoody. "Not at all. I just ... didn't sleep much, did you?"

"No," I admit. Did Cole stay awake seeing Frank's body, too? I think of the bloody rock in his hand. "That's why I asked Taylor to swap. I mean, that was one of the reasons. I thought we could talk about it." I'm sure his face just grew a little paler. "You know, if you wanted to."

"Maybe later," he says slowly. "After the tour? I think I need to take my mind off it for a bit."

"Sure, later. Listen, we can skip the tour if you want. It's only because you didn't get to come to an open evening, that's all."

"Are you kidding? I've been looking forward to this. I've only really seen the science lab and my room this

97

week, it's been a bit of a whirlwind." A smile tickles the corners of his mouth. "Even more now you're here."

I flush. "No pressure, then." I gesture to the doors and hope he can't see how embarrassed I am. "After you."

"Wait a second, I've always wanted to do this. . ." He grabs one polished doorknob in each hand and counts under his breath before throwing both doors open in unison and they swing inwards. "You may enter. . . Oh, wow."

"I know, right?"

Morton's library is what I dreamed libraries should look like when I was a little kid: nothing like the shabby bookshelves at my underfunded primary school. All three facing walls are decorated with floor-to-ceiling windows. Each has a "reading nook" built in and they are punctuated throughout with bookshelves that soar up to the high ceiling. The ceiling is a work of art itself, all original beams and plaster ceiling roses. They even have those massive ladders on wheels so you can get to the books right at the top – I swear I will have my *Beauty and the Beast* moment before I leave.

Cole starts to cross the polished black and white tiles, pausing to brush a hand over the study benches in the centre of the room and finally stopping to snap the toggle of a lamp on and off.

"It's like something out of a film," he whispers loudly, his library voice. I smile.

"I know, that's what I thought when I first saw it, too. The little green lights and everything."

"Yeah. I feel like I'm in New York Public Library or something. It's so cool." He wanders further into the room and I can't help but feel a little pride that it's me showing him this. "Hey." He stops at a squat glass cabinet in the centre of the room. "What's all this?"

"Those are Morton's 'curiosities'," I tell him, coming closer. "Things that the founder had in his collection when he started the school. Old white guys love to collect stuff on their adventures. Some of it's a bit politically incorrect, I reckon, but it's all pretty fascinating."

"There's more?

"Yeah, look." I gesture around the room to the cabinets at the end of every study bench and in front of each reading nook. "It'll take ages to see everything, but I can show you some of my favourites?"

"Yeah, sure."

"This one," I point at a small, black disc, "is made from obsidian – see how shiny it is? Apparently it was used by magicians to scry the future. You know, see visions and stuff."

He laughs. "Visions? Bet they made them all up. I mean, it's just an extrusive rock. It's made from cooled lava."

"Maybe they did." I stare at the glassy surface. "I wonder if it ever really worked."

"Probably not," Cole laughs and I straighten up. "I'm a scientist, remember? Come on, what else have we got?"

"Let's go over here." I lead him to the furthest cabinet from the double doors, at the opposite side of the room below a huge stained-glass window. "I love this one." I point to what looks like an open book, made of wood – only there are no pages inside it. Instead, there are little drawers. "This was owned by the Poisoner of Dusseldorf, back in the 1780s. See these hidden drawers? They had plants like belladonna in them. He used to take a lover and kill them slowly, then move on to another and another... Grim, right?" Cole nods, his lips tight. "Guess what the outside of the book looks like."

"Please don't tell me it's the Bible?"

"Got it in one. They think it was shipped over from Germany in the late 1800s, along with Old Josef."

"Who's Old Josef?"

Oops.

"One of those guys." I think quickly, pointing to a nearby cabinet full of phrenology heads, which I know are *definitely* problematic. "The psychology kids name them all."

"Weirdos." He smiles at me. "You do classics, but what else? I know we're not doing the same subjects, I didn't see you all week."

"Yeah, classics. I love it. I do modern history and art, too. Anything old tickles my geek weak point, and I love to be creative, I find it really soothing. A bit different from science – I'm just good at 'interpreting' stuff. You are a properly clever person."

"Guilty." He laughs and holds a hand up. "I find natural poisons pretty fascinating, you know? It's like, nature's own defence system."

"I guess so."

"How about one more and then we can hit the dining room for breakfast, right? That has to be on the tour. I'm starved."

"Deal," I say. I glance around, trying to decide, but Cole chooses first. He walks over to a cabinet with just one item in it and calls, "What's this one?"

"You've chosen my all-time favourite." I smile as I stop in front of the glass case. Inside is a terracotta sculpture, a tiny, glorious angel, its face worn and blank, the skeleton of its wire wings poking through, poised to take flight. Ancient pieces of clay have crumbled from the innards and the whole effect is morbidly beautiful. "It's a Bernini."

"Bernini was a sculptor, right?"

I smile and nod, delighted he has heard of him. "He was. Most of his work is in the Vatican, but this little one was an early study for the angels on the Ponte Sant'Angelo in Rome. You ever been?" He shakes his head. "Me neither," I admit, "but I dream about it. Bernini sculpted these beautiful angels, all of them perfect, flawless. They're stunning. I prefer this, though, his early prototype. You can see the raw ideas and it's so moving – broken, flawed but still so beautiful." I stop, embarrassed, feeling Cole's eyes on me. "Sorry. Told you – history nerd."

"Don't apologize. You just look pretty when you're so animated, that's all." He stops. "Sorry, I'm making it weird."

"No, you're not." I smile up at him as a slice of sunlight cuts through the room and lands perfectly on the sculpture. "All right, then," I say, smiling even wider. "Breakfast?"

I point out the common rooms as we leave, right opposite the entrance to the library and promise to bring him back later; they officially open to us today. The dining hall is over at the opposite end of school and we walk there in silence, but it's a nice silence. Comfortable. We follow the smell of toast into the hall, which is predictably rammed, and join the queue for breakfast. It's all so Morton, when I try to look through fresh eyes, like Cole must be. Long tables behind which uniformed kitchen staff serve. Crisp, white tablecloths and piles of food in baskets and on silver serving dishes.

He grins. "This is a bit different from during the week! Look at all this. It's like a hotel breakfast, isn't it?"

"It is?" I've never had a hotel breakfast. "They do this every Saturday and Sunday. Beats the DIY cereal stations we usually have."

"Does it ever!" Cole starts piling stuff on to his plate as

we reach the front of the queue and I watch as he charms the serving staff into giving him double of everything. I select my own food carefully, avoiding anything that might trigger a headache, and pour myself a glass of orange juice.

"Want one?" I ask Cole, who nods without tearing his eyes away from the pastry stand. I pour a second and balance both little glasses in one hand. "Come on, then."

He reluctantly follows me away from the food as I weave through the dining hall, heading for our table. All the seats are refectory style – long, wooden counters lined with long, wooden benches. I reach the corner where Taylor, Kat and Marcus are already huddled and gesture for Cole to grab his glass off me. I put my own breakfast down and climb into the seat next to Kat, as Cole settles himself opposite me, next to Marcus.

"Morning, sunshine." Taylor smiles at me over a half-eaten yogurt but it doesn't reach her eyes. "How're you feeling?"

"OK," I say and study the top of my own raspberry yogurt before peeling the foil lid back and scraping the thick, creamy gloop off with my spoon. "How're you, Kat? Sleep much?"

"Not really," she mumbles from behind a steaming cup of coffee, "hence the caffeine. This week has been something else, hasn't it? I'm half afraid to go to sleep in case . . . oh I don't know. In case something else happens, I guess." She lifts her cup and wrinkles her nose at the smell.

"I don't even like the stuff but I need to hit the gym this morning."

"Me too," says Marcus. "I'll come with if you don't wanna be on your own. I'll test you on your PB while you quiz me on covalent bonds."

Kat smiles wickedly. She loves being underestimated. "Bring it on."

"You wanna come, Cole?" Marcus mops up the remains of his breakfast with a piece of toast as he talks and I wonder how they have such big appetites after last night. I look down at the red flecks in my pink yogurt and feel my stomach turn. I push it away.

"No, thanks, maybe tomorrow. Liz here is giving me the big Morton tour today," Cole answers. I'm grateful he wants to stick with me; I need the distraction after what happened last night. I can't deal with it yet.

"We've just seen the library," I explain. "I thought we'd do the whole loop and meet you guys back in the common room for lunch?"

"Sounds good to me," Kat says, downing the dregs of her coffee and stretching. "I need a few hours of normal before everyone starts asking us about last night." She shakes her head. "Did you see the cop car parked out front this morning? I reckon we might get hauled in for questioning at some point. I still can't believe it happened."

"What?" I didn't see a car this morning, it must have arrived after I met Cole and I was too busy chatting to him on the way back to notice. The buzz in the air suddenly becomes more noticeable. People are talking about it.

"Yeah. I don't think anyone has been told yet, but it won't be long. It's not every day there's a police presence at school. I'm going to try and enjoy the normal while it lasts."

"You're right," I agree softly. "A few hours of normality would be nice." I sip my orange juice but it's bitter and pulpy, so I put that down, too. I'll fill up my water bottle on the way out. "What're you doing today, Tay?"

"Homework," she sighs. "No Saturday's off for me this year, even with everything that's going on. You'd think Patel would give me the day off after last night, but open evening approaches and my head girl duties are on a Sunday, so I have to get it all finished today. I'll still meet you guys for lunch, though, I'll need the brainfood. Say oneish?"

I look at the clock over the doorway – ten fifteen – and nod. "Sounds good to me, gives us plenty of time. That OK with you, Cole?"

He looks up through a forkful of scrambled egg and nods, swallowing.

"You think I've got time for seconds?"

17

"I thought we'd start out here in the grounds and then finish with the rest of the house on the way back for lunch?"

"Sure." Cole follows me out of the main doors and I pause to inhale the smell of the rose and lavender gardens on either side, my favourite scents. They soothe my soul and I open my eyes, ready to begin.

"This way." I walk down the path to the large turning circle in front of the house. It's like one of those driveways you see on films about royalty, where they drive right up to the front door. There's even a fountain in the middle.

The police car looks out of place in front of it.

"No way. You think they will want to talk to us today?"

"Probably. We were at the crime scene."

We walk past the car in silence. It's empty of people but the seats are littered with food wrappers, the footwell on the passenger side full of paper coffee cups. The officers must be inside school. I shiver.

"I still can't get over how wild this place is," Cole says after a few seconds, as if to break the tension. Our feet crunch on the gravel as we veer off to the right and circle back around the side of the building. The columns that form a kind of veranda all the way around Morton line one side and the library peers out at us. Cole nods, recognizing where he is, getting his bearings.

On the other side, tall hedges loom over us, twice the size of me. "This place is ridiculous," Cole murmurs.

"I know what you mean. How the other half live, right?" I stop in front of a tall iron fence that punctures the hedge row. "I'll show you out here and then we can go round the back of the house."

To the lake. But I don't say that out loud.

The gate is open, as usual, and Cole follows me beyond the hedges and on to a short, manicured lawn. We follow the path and stop in front of a car park. It's full of boring cars, apart from Mr Lucas's convertible BMW. He's definitely having a mid-life crisis.

"Nothing too exciting this side, but worth knowing about. Teachers' car park here and that" – I point to a large

building that was once a barn or an outhouse of some kind –
"is the teachers' living quarters."

"They all live here, too?"

"Not all of them, but yeah, some. Most of the staff who
have families live in Prescott. It's the nearest town with
decent schools and transport, but it's almost an hour away,
so some choose to live on site. Dr Patel does, but she has
her own entrance and quarters as far as I know." We weave
through the parked cars and follow a short road that leads
to yet more gates. "This is the staff entrance, for deliveries
to the kitchen and stuff." I pause and point over to the far
side, away from the house. "There are stables there if you
like horses. I tried riding last year and, er, let's say it wasn't
one of the things I'm good at."

Cole grins. "I am clearly going to need you to tell me
this story."

"Another time." I laugh, remembering the horse
bolting while I clung on for dear life. "Not enough
time gone for it to be funny yet. Anyway," I continue,
ignoring his sexy little smirk, "there's a paddock and an
allotment – the school is really big on organic, home-
grown fruit and veg – and Creepy Billy's place is over
there, too."

"Wait – I'm sorry. Creepy who now?"

I give Cole my best wicked grin and lower my voice.
"Creepy Billy, the groundskeeper. You met him last
night." He squints nervously past the greenhouses as

though he can magic him up by staring. "He always skulks around, carrying this long-handled fork." I drop my voice to a whisper. "They say he sharpens it every night, on the corner of an old gravestone."

"Awesome," Cole breathes and I can't help it, I start to giggle. "Wait, are you having me on?"

"Kind of," I admit. "I mean, I have heard those stories, but he just seems like a nice old guy. He avoids us mostly – I don't blame him."

"Yeah, that's sad. Let's be nice if we see him."

"Deal." He is so sweet, I just can't. "Right, let's go see the fun stuff."

"Lead the way." He holds an arm out and I lead us back through the gate in the hedge and continue around the back of the school building. We don't stop chatting the whole way – he tells me about home, how he lives with his mum and younger sister. I don't ask about his dad and he doesn't volunteer the information, but there's pain behind his eyes when he talks about them.

We pass around the back and I point out the common rooms and kitchens, then the dining hall. We finally reach another gate, a mirror image of the last one, and beyond it I see a sparkle of blue water. The lake is out this way.

I take a deep breath and step through.

"Hey." Cole puts a gentle hand on my shoulder. "Are you OK? You don't look so good."

"Of course." I try to force a note of brightness into my

voice, but it falls flat. "So, this is the lake." We look out at the large expanse of water. A path surrounds the whole thing and from here we can see a few people jogging around the far side. "The running club," I point out. "You like to run?"

"Nah, I get bored." Cole smiles. "Football is my thing." I roll my eyes. "Hey, it's the sport of royalty – twenty-two kings playing on a field of gold."

"Oh, please." I'm only half listening to him, though. My eyes keep drifting back to the little pier halfway between us and the far side of the lake, where a bunch of kayaks and canoes are moored. Cole follows my gaze.

"What is it?"

I take a deep breath. "Do you know why you got a place in second year? I mean, aside from you being super clever, which you must be."

"Yeah, I heard a kid died. Morgan, the old head girl? I felt a bit weird about it, to be honest. Like I was taking her place. The first thing I did when I got the offer was Google Morton, so I already knew that much."

"Well, yeah. Morgan died out here, on the lake." I swallow hard, the words sticking in my throat. "*We* were out here."

"We? What, like you and her? God, Liz, I'm so sorry. I did wonder when you said you'd banged your head in an accident but I didn't want to pry. What happened?"

I can almost see that night playing out in front of me, a

faded film reel projecting on to the still water. "It was a . . . dare. To take the boats out at night." An *initiation* is what Morgan called it. "It was the last day of term. We'd been drinking and Morgan was showing off." My voice trails away and my fingers automatically find the scar in my hair.

"Hey, stop. You don't have to tell me." Cole's hand is on my shoulder again and I feel the heat of his skin seep through my T-shirt.

I glance up at him. "I don't really remember much more, anyway." I lower my head and part my hair so he can see the scar properly and I hear his sharp intake of breath. I flick my hair back and smile weakly. "The boat flipped. I got this and she . . . didn't make it back."

"I'm so sorry." His hand is still on my shoulder and he lets it slide down my arm, his warm fingers wrapping around my own. "You were pretty lucky, then."

"Yeah." I squeeze his hand and drop it gently, embarrassed. He is too sweet. "Come on, let's check out the sports fields."

Cole is way too into the football field, enthusing about the pitch and the stands and wittering on about goalposts and penalty boxes. I let him talk, though, enjoying the feeling of release that has settled over me. I'd been holding that night in all summer and finally confronting it, seeing the lake again, has made me feel lighter than I have in weeks.

We walk around the cages that enclose the hockey,

netball and tennis courts and loop back towards the lake path. "One more stop," I tell him, pointing at a low building that sits behind the netball court, "and then we can head back for lunch."

"Perfect. This must be the gym then, right? Marcus told me it was out here."

"Yeah." We head into the foyer. It's pretty busy in there, mainly lads sitting around between sets, but over in the far corner, by the water cooler, are Marcus and Kat.

"Jeez, she can bench more than me!" Cole splutters. I grin. Kat is lying on a bench, her feet firmly planted on the floor, pushing a weighted iron bar into the air. Huge, black discs hang on each side and I see Cole mentally totting up the weights. He nods in awe. "*Definitely* more than me."

"Hey, guys!" I wave as Marcus helps Kat place the barbell in its rest. She slides out and waves, grabbing her bottle of water off the floor before heading over to us.

"That was pretty impressive," Cole says to her.

"What, for a girl?"

"Hell no, for anyone. I'm impressed."

"She still hasn't beaten my PB, though," Marcus says, sidling up behind her. Kat rolls her eyes. I swear if she had a towel she would whip him with it.

"Give me time." She drains her bottle. "Speaking of time, is it almost lunch yet?"

"Almost twelve, we're heading back to finish the tour now then collapsing in the common room. Coming?"

Kat holds the damp fabric of her grey top away from her skin and shakes her head. "I need a shower, but we'll see you there."

"Yeah, same. Meet you in the common room." Marcus agrees. He and Kat head over to the showers, ribbing each other good-naturedly on the way.

Cole and I leave the gym and start back on the path to the lake. The early autumn sun casts golden rays across the water and I relish its warmth as we stroll along in comfortable silence.

"Do they have a bit of a thing going on or what?" Cole interrupts my moment of zen.

"Who? What – Marcus and Kat?" I start laughing. "God, no. Marcus and Taylor are practically married. He would never. He and Kat are more like brother and sister than anything. And Kat is. . ."

"Is she gay? Or bi?"

"What, because she can lift weights?" I tease him.

"Hell no, I'm no misogynist." Good to know. "I saw her snogging that girl in the crop top last night, the one she'd been drinking shots . . . er, from. . ."

"Ha! Typical Kat." I can't help but smile. "She's . . . not really into relationships." I shrug. "She likes who she likes – and she hates labels."

"Fair enough." He gives me a sidelong glance. "What about you? Are you into relationships? Or, to be even more blunt – is there someone I should be worried about?"

I duck my head, allowing a short curtain of hair to hide my face. "No, no one special."

"Cool." His fingers fold around mine again.

This time I don't let go.

18

The common room is already packed when we get back to the main building, and I watch as Cole's eyes widen at the lunch spread. It's not too dissimilar from breakfast this morning, but it's a huge senior privilege – the juniors eat in the dining room as we usually do.

"Yes," is all he says.

I've got to admit, I'm feeling pretty hungry myself after our mooch around the grounds this morning. I didn't get much exercise over the holidays, our estate isn't exactly one you want to walk around alone, and I can feel the muscles in my legs already starting to ache. Maybe I should take Kat up on her gym offer, after all. Eww – I feel sweaty just thinking about it.

"What's the plan?" Cole asks, eyes still firmly on the covered silver platters.

"Come on," I say. "Let's find somewhere to sit."

The common room is long and slender. Windows pierce the long wall, just like in the library, but the light doesn't streak in the same way. Instead we can see the tall hedgerows that separate us from the staff car park – the path Cole and I took earlier. The decor is similar to the lounge upstairs, essentially Morton – wood-panelled walls, highly polished surfaces and comfy, battered leather chairs. The space is filled with sofas and seating areas where low-slung armchairs are arranged around old leather chests and wooden boxes that double as coffee tables. It's pretty similar to the juniors' common room, though that has hardly any windows.

A huge stone fireplace dominates the wall in the centre of the room and three worn, green sofas are wrapped around it. It immediately marks itself out as the most coveted spot in the room and I grin when I spot Taylor's red hair streaming over the arm of a couch.

"Amazing," I say as we join her and she grins up from her prostrate position. "How long have you been here?"

"Ages," she says, pulling herself into an upright position. "I came in as soon as I saw them open the doors from the library and pretended to be asleep so no one would join me. Gotta mark out my territory now I'm head girl, right?"

"Legend." Cole smiles. I take a seat on the sofa opposite Taylor and, even though there's a third one facing the fireplace, he sits next to me. Taylor raises an eyebrow and I shoot her a warning look.

"Good tour, was it?" she asks innocently.

"Yeah, this place is amazing, I love it. And my tour guide wasn't bad either, so thanks for that." Taylor's grin is in danger of straining a cheek muscle as Cole gets to his feet. "The food is out! I'm gonna go grab something. Liz, you want anything?"

I shake my head. "No. I'll go up in a bit, thanks."

"Taylor?"

"No, we'll keep the seats. You go ahead."

We follow his tall frame as Marcus and Kat come in through the double doors, both scrubbed and clean looking. Marcus joins Cole in the queue, slapping his back as Kat comes over to us, swinging her gym bag on to the floor and sprawling on the spare sofa.

"Well, well, well." Taylor fixes her gaze on me like the proverbial cat that got the canary. "Sounds like Liz had a nice morning with the new boy."

"Yes, thank you," I say primly. They look at me expectantly. "He's great. Too good for me, though," I confess.

"What?!" Kat squeals, drawing glances as she leans forwards. She doesn't lower her voice, though, that's not her style. "Lizzie, you're the best. You deserve the best.

And, well." She leers over to where Cole and Marcus are piling food on to their plates. "He is pretty damn close."

I bite my lip. The idea that such a handsome, kind, funny new boy would like *me*, straight off the bat ... it doesn't feel possible, somehow. Things like that just don't happen to me.

"Kat!" I can't help but laugh as she wiggles her eyebrows. "Stop being such a deviant. But, yeah, I like him." I put a hand to my head. "He's really calming to talk to," I say at last.

"And he is capital H Hot," Taylor says, as Kat nods her agreement. I let my gaze drift and see Cole walking back over. He flashes me a smile and I return it.

After lunch, the chest that masquerades as a table is littered with the remnants and I watch, mesmerized, as Taylor methodically scrapes leftovers on to one plate before piling them all up and placing the cutlery on top. "Once a waitress," she mutters, as Marcus grabs the stack from her and carries them back to the staff at the other end of the room. Cole nudges me and whispers in my ear.

"You were right," he says, "they are totally a married couple."

The room is quieter now, as most people have gone off to hang out on the lawn in the sunshine, but I'm comfy here. I feel myself getting sleepy – I could doze off right here, with Cole's arm resting gently behind me. I sink lower in my seat, eyes heavy, and it feels natural when Cole slips an arm around my shoulder. I hesitate for a second but then I relax into him, just a little.

Marcus sits back down next to Taylor and lowers his voice. "Does anyone else know about Frank yet?"

"I don't know," I say. I look around at the other students, eating and chatting. "It all feels a bit surreal. Like, if you two hadn't been with me, I'd think I dreamed it."

"Yeah, I know what you mean," Cole agrees, withdrawing his arm, much to my disappointment. He mimics Marcus's pose, closing our little group. "No one has mentioned it *at all*. You would think it's big news but nothing. When Jameela ... died ... it's all anyone could talk about in lessons, right?" We nod in agreement.

"I guess we've barely seen anyone this morning, though," I say. "Tay, was there any chatter in the library?"

"I don't think so." She flicks her eyes up to the ceiling, thinking. "I saw his room-mates in the library, but they didn't seem too concerned. After his outburst earlier this week maybe they think he was finally sent home."

"Wouldn't they be worried?" Kat asks. "If one of you didn't come back one night, I'd worry, especially if there were police around."

Cole shrugs. "Maybe they've been in with Patel all morning. I guess they could be here for anything. And the whole not going home thing – guys might not think much of it. They might think he ... well, stayed out late or something." He flushes and I realize that "or something" means "hooked up".

Taylor is frowning. "Patel's covered it up, hasn't she? Three student deaths in less than eight weeks can't look great for the school."

There's a murmur of agreement as we all sit and contemplate what a bad reputation for Morton might mean for our futures. We're quiet for a moment, and then I think of something. "Kat?" I ask, my voice low. "Do you still have the inhaler?"

"Inhaler?" Taylor repeats. "What inhaler?"

"Jameela's inhaler," Kat says. She rifles through her gym bag and pulls out a plastic sandwich bag. Sealed inside is Jameela's pink inhaler. "These guys found it in Frank's hand. I wanted to preserve the evidence." She says it so seriously that none of us even think to laugh. "It's all a bit intense, isn't it? I mean, first Jameela. . ."

"Are we saying that Jameela's death wasn't an accident?" Taylor says. "But surely – I mean, she was smoking . . . it was just one of those things. . ."

"Why did Frank have it, then?" Kat asks, placing the bag on the table. We all stare at it. "Patel said he must have fallen and hit his head. Do we believe that?"

"Well, I certainly don't." Another voice crashes our private conversation.

I swear, our heads all whip around at the exact same moment, as though some unseen puppet master has just tugged at our strings. We turn as a figure behind us gets to her feet.

"You know, it's rude to eavesdrop," Taylor snarls as Emily walks around and stands in the gap between the sofas.

"Oh, please – like Kat knows anything about discretion. Do you want to hear what I've got to say or not?"

Kat shrugs, apparently taking no offence at practically being called a loudmouth, and gestures to the empty seat next to her.

The rest of us aren't as laid-back – Cole stiffens next to my bouncing knee, Taylor looks like she might throw up and tension is emanating from Marcus across the table. We could really do without our little Agatha Christie act getting back to the headmistress. Emily doesn't seem to notice any of it as she perches on the edge of the seat, her watery eyes fixed on the inhaler. She's lost her two best friends in a matter of weeks. It would be like losing Taylor and Kat. I shiver.

"What do you want to say?" I ask gently. "Go ahead." There's a wobble in my voice and Cole takes my hand again.

"Jameela's *accidental* death. First off, how come there was no memorial, like there was for Morgan? People aren't even talking about it. Well, it's all bull, isn't it? All cloak and dagger."

"People are talking about her, of course they are,"

Marcus says uncertainly. "No one *official* has said anything, though, have they? No formal assembly, no mention of her at all apart from Patel saying her family wanted to keep it all private. Do you know what I think?" Emily asks.

We all stare at her.

"Jameela's parents adored her, but they had nothing. That's why she was so desperate to be head girl. They'd want some kind of compensation."

"You're saying Patel . . . paid them not to ask questions?" Marcus says.

"Yeah. It's like she just disappeared. Like she was never even here." Emily nods at the inhaler. "Jameela knew she shouldn't smoke – she knew her asthma could get really bad. But the inhaler should have helped her. I've seen her use it so many times and it always helped, so the fact that she . . . that she . . ."

We all sit in silence, not sure what to do or say. I stare down at the worn rug beneath the coffee chest, tracing its faded patterns with my eyes until I feel dizzy. I remember Jameela taking deep breaths of the inhaler. *It should have helped her.*

Emily blinks back tears. "Now you're saying that Frank is dead? And he had this with him?"

I risk a glance up. Every face is sombre and there are tears streaking down Emily's cheeks. No one speaks.

"Well?" she demands quietly. "Is it true? Is Frank dead, too?"

"Yes," I croak. I clear my voice and try again. "Yes. We found him last night, on the way back from the party."

"Who did?" Emily asks sharply. "You?"

I nod.

"Actually, it was me," Cole says, his voice small. "I found him. He was already ... his head." Cole swallows and closes his eye. I squeeze his fingers.

"And me." Kat picks up the plastic bag. "And it's true, he was holding this. So the question is why? Why did Frank have Jameela's inhaler?"

Emily laughs, a hollow, humourless sound. "Isn't it obvious?" She looks around at us, stares into the faces of each of my friends. "So much for the brightest and the best." She slows her speech down, like she's talking to a group of small children. "There's something wrong with that inhaler and Frank knew it. Someone poisoned my friend and he found out. Then whoever it was killed him too."

None of us say anything for a moment.

"I knew it!" Kat hisses. "Something is going on and we have to do something about it. Oh, God. What do we do?"

"Wait a second." Marcus holds up a hand, the voice of reason. "We don't know any of this is true. Maybe Jameela *just* had an asthma attack and Frank *just* fell in the woods. It's sad and, yeah, unusual, but that's all it is. There's no evidence we have a *killer* here."

"Prove it, then." Emily folds her arms defiantly.

"Prove what?" he says, bewildered. "That it's unusual?"

"No, you idiot," Emily responds coldly. "Prove the inhaler isn't poisoned."

"How am I supposed to do that?"

"You're a scientist, aren't you?" She says it accusingly, like it's a bad thing. "Then test the inhaler. Test it and prove my best friend wasn't murdered."

"Tell me again what we're actually doing here." I squirm on the hard wooden stool, trying for the seventeenth time to get comfortable.

"Don't bother." Marcus looks up from the cupboard he's rummaging in. "I think they're made to be uncomfortable on purpose. Ah." He straightens up and shuts the door with one foot. "Here, put these on."

"You've got to be kidding." I stare at the clear plastic safety goggles he puts in my hand.

"Nope, science lab rules – safety first."

I throw a sidelong glance at Cole, who shrugs and puts on his own scratched-up pair. "Man's right. Come on, get them on." I give Kat one last, hopeful look of rebellion, but she's already wearing hers and vogueing into the reflection of a glass cabinet. I bet Taylor wouldn't wear them if she was here.

"Come on, Lizzie, suit up!" she demands. I sigh and slide the glasses over the bridge of my nose where they give me an immediate headache.

"Fine," I grumble. "Now, answer my question. What are we doing?"

"Gas chromatography–mass spectroscopy," Marcus replies. Cole nods, his eyes lighting up. Kat plays with the gas taps mounted on the centre of the table and Marcus slaps her hands away playfully. She frowns.

"Which is what?"

"A way of seeing if there's anything in that inhaler that shouldn't be."

"Right," I reply, casting my mind back to high-school science, "so you need to separate the components somehow? How do we do that?"

Kat looks up, her hands on the gas taps again. "Please tell me it's the thing with the Bunsen burners where you set stuff on fire and it goes different colours."

"Er, not quite, and if you keep messing with those you're going to end up with no eyebrows." Marcus places the plastic bag containing Jameela's inhaler on the table and gestures to the canister through the plastic. "Everything in here should be a liquid. It's kept in a compressed chamber, so when the pump is activated it lets out a small, measured amount that becomes a gas at body temp. We need to make sure that everything in there *should* be in there. I asked Mr Lucas if we could have access to the gas chromatography machine this afternoon and. . ."

Kat cuts him off. "What? You told a teacher about this?"

"No, of course not!" Marcus cuts her off. For a moment, I think I see real anger on his face, but the look is gone so quickly I might have imagined it. "No, Cole and I told him we wanted to up our game a bit, for uni applications." He points at a hulking white machine in the corner. "You only really get these at degree level, but you know Morton. No expense spared. Just another bonus point on our applications." He picks up the bag. "Cole, give me a hand?"

"Sure." Cole eases long legs from the stool and I watch him approach the machine.

"Not that Mr Head Boy needs the points," Kat whispers in my ear. "Anyway, I thought that was the photocopier." I stifle a laugh, ignoring the barbed comment. That's not like Kat, it's just the stress of the whole situation.

"Me too," I admit. "Come on, let's see what they're doing."

Kat and I stand back slightly as we watch the boys work. "Can you believe Taylor knows how to do all this stuff, too?" She says in awe. "Girl's a total knockout *and* a genius. Makes me proud."

"Me too." I smile, nodding towards the boys. "How

come all the science kids are hotties? My classics class is severely lacking..." I stop suddenly, realizing there'll be two empty seats there tomorrow morning. First Jameela and now Frank, gone.

"Hey." Kat squeezes my hand. It's like she can read my mind. "This is why we're here, to try and help. To get some evidence."

"Who would we even show it to?" I say, in a small voice.

"We'll show it to someone," Kat says firmly and I nod. We turn our attention back to Marcus and Cole. Marcus gingerly takes the inhaler from the bag and twists the silver cylinder, separating it from the plastic casing. A familiar smell drifts through the air, something menthol, but I can't quite place it. "Can you smell that?" I ask Kat.

"What? Oh." She pauses to take a sniff of her Fleetwood Mac T-shirt. "This?" I inhale the fabric.

"Yeah. I thought it was from the inhaler for a sec."

"No, it's me. Tiger Balm," she explains, lowering her voice. "Lifting those weights with Marcus yesterday did me in, but don't tell him, will you? I'm in agony today, think I pulled a lat."

I nod sympathetically, even though I can't remember what a lat is. "Your secret's safe with me."

"Thanks." Kat addresses the boys. "How long will this take?"

"About an hour, I think," Cole replies, his eyes on the syringe in Marcus's hand. Marcus nods his agreement and narrows his dark eyes, inserting the sharp needle into the tiny opening at the bottom of the cylinder.

"Hold still," he murmurs and we watch in rapt silence. When he's sure it's all in place, he starts to pull back the end of the syringe slowly, filling the small chamber with a tiny amount of liquid. Satisfied, he removes the needle. "Is there enough in there for a second go if this doesn't work?"

Cole holds the canister up to his ear and shakes it. Guess we're past worrying about fingerprints. "Yeah, sounds like there is."

"Good." Marcus walks back to the machine and starts to press buttons. A low whirring sound fills the room and he begins making checks with Cole. "Carrier gas ready?"

Cole checks a section at the end and nods. "Yep."

"OK, I'm going to put this into the injector port." Marcus glances up at us, kicking into teacher mode. "Once this goes in, it'll travel around the column, which is like a long, twisty glass tube, and then the components will start to separate. The chemicals with the highest boiling points will eluate – sorry, come out – first and once it's done, we should have the results of what's in here."

"All right then." I nod and we watch as he once again inserts the syringe needle, this time into a port on the top of the machine.

"What do we do while we wait?" I ask.

Kat sighs and looks back at her heavy bag. "Homework."

*

129

"What was that?" A short series of beeps sounds and I tear my eyes away from a book about the Parthenon that's been keeping me distracted.

"The results." Cole looks me in the eye. "They're ready."

A cold, hollow feeling starts to spread in the pit of my stomach. It's the moment of truth. I say a silent prayer to whichever gods might be listening. I want the results to show that nothing unusual was in the inhaler. Just a tragic accident, that's all. Then things could get back to normal.

But I'm not sure they ever will.

"Let's all go look together," Kat says. Marcus nods and stands up, the metal legs of his stool scraping across the hard floor.

We walk over to the machine hesitantly. There's a computer screen linked up to the apparatus and it is flashing, telling us it's ready to reveal its secrets. I take a deep breath as Cole's hand closes around mine on one side and Kat's does the same on the other, forming a human chain, and I relax slightly. Marcus drags a stool in front of the monitor and quickly taps on the keyboard.

Over his shoulder I can see a line graph full of little peaks, like I imagine a lie detector must look like, or a Richter scale. Three large ones stand out from the others.

Marcus points at the screen. "OK, so these peaks represent the ions present in the liquid from the inhaler. We can ignore the smaller ones – they're just trace elements from the air and whatever. We want to focus on the big ones, then we interpret and try to identify them."

"So what's in there?" I ask.

"I'm not sure." He runs a large hand over the back of his head, scratching at the short bristles there. "I can't tell you the generic names without looking them up, I'm not so hot on those. I can tell you the pharmaceutical names, though."

Cole drops my hand to retrieve the inhaler, now reassembled and back in the bag. He twists the canister through the plastic and peers at the label. "Right, you tell me what you think they are."

"OK, so . . . first one is beclometasone dipropionate," Marcus reads from the screen.

"Yep, got that." Cole nods as he squints at the tiny writing. "Next?"

"Formorterol fumarate?" My gaze flits between the two boys, like I'm watching a tennis match. Beside me, Kat does the same.

"Er, wait a sec. . . Oh, yeah, it's here. Got it."

"You want the third?"

"Yeah." Cole peels apart the seal on the bag and removes the inhaler. "Sorry, can't see it through the bag. Go ahead."

"OK, so the third is . . . trimethylbicyclo heptan."

I hold my breath, waiting for Cole to confirm that it's an ingredient in the inhaler. "Jeez," Kat whispers.

Cole reads the label carefully. Then he looks up slowly and shakes his head.

"No." His voice is hoarse and he drops the inhaler back into the bag. "No. There are only two ingredients on here. That's definitely not one of them."

"I don't believe it." Marcus turns on his stool, his shoulders sagging. "You know what this means?"

I nod, swallowing hard. The very words I'm thinking spill out of Kat's mouth.

"It means there was something in Jameela's inhaler that shouldn't have been there. It means that Emily was right." Kat looks at me, fear barely hidden in her thickly lashed eyes. "Someone killed Jameela and Frank knew it, so someone killed him, too."

"It's worse than that," Marcus says softly. "It means it was one of us."

"What did he mean, *one of us*?"

Taylor's snuggled in her old dorm bed, catching up on our news. Outside the door we can hear sobs, the patter of feet from one room to another. Frank's death is common knowledge now – another tragic accident at Morton Academy. Taylor looks tired, her face washed clean of make-up so her brows and lashes are pale. There's a red, inflamed mark on her cheekbone.

"Not one of *us* exactly, but someone here, at Morton." Kat responds between sit-ups, her feet hooked under my bed.

"Well, duh. Who else is it going to be? Bless him, he's

not always the fastest on the uptake, is he? Maybe we should go and see Patel, tell her what we know. I mean, I'm head girl, we're all Jewel and Bone acolytes. There's got to be some level of trust there. She'll have our backs, surely?"

"I don't know anything any more." I sigh. I'm holding a bag of sweets, but I've lost my appetite. "We think she bribed that police officer after all."

"She might just be protecting the school; I bet the governors were a nightmare after Morgan's death was in the papers last July."

"Maybe." I shrug.

"Well, I'm out of big ideas. Here, pass me some of those, will you?" I throw Taylor a mini bag of Haribo. She nods at Kat. "Why does watching her exercise just make me crave sugar?"

"Wait a sec," I say, "haven't you spoken to Marcus today?"

"No, can you believe it?" Taylor slides a jelly ring on to her finger and starts to nibble at it. "Patel kept me busy with head girl stuff all day. It wasn't even fun Jewel and Bone party stuff, just open evening rubbish. There's going to be prospective donors there or something so I had to draw up a timetable for the tours."

"I forgot it was open evening so soon."

I think back to the day I landed on the doorstep at Morton. It took my breath away – I'd never seen anything like it. I'd sat a handful of my exams early and Dr Patel had come to interview me at my high school. She offered me a place on the spot, and I came on my own to see if it was real.

I had been saving up the money I got washing hair at my secret Saturday job, so I used it for the train ticket and didn't tell anyone. It was love at first sight and I couldn't get here fast enough after that. My parents have never seen it, not that they'd be interested anyway. They signed the paperwork, which made things less difficult, but if they knew what it was really like, they'd just say I thought I was better than them or something.

"Do you have to do the tours and stuff?" I ask now.

"Yeah, I think we all do, actually." Taylor rips the head off a small bear with her perfect white teeth and puts on a big, fake smile as Kat collapses back on the carpet. "Hi, hello," Taylor chirps, "welcome to Morton Academy, the exclusive, scholarship-only school for super clever students, where people are dropping like flies!" Her voice breaks on the last word as she sniffs back a sob.

"Oh, hon. We can't panic, not now," Kat says from the floor, her cropped tee showing off enviable abs. "We just have to put a brave face on it, for a little while anyway."

"Kat's right," I agree, carefully folding my little plastic packet. "We have to keep our heads down, at least until we know who we can and can't trust."

"God, is this for real?" Taylor burrows down under the duvet. "How did we end up in this mess? I mean first

Morgan, then Jameela and now poor Frank – I mean he was a bit weird and all, but he didn't deserve to die."

"No, of course he didn't," Kat says soothingly, as she climbs into her own bed. "No one deserves that. I just have so many questions."

I scooch back in my bed. "Like what?" I ask, feeling a slight stirring of interest under all my worry. Kat is smart, after all.

"OK." Kat begins to count on her fingers. "First off, why didn't whoever poisoned Jameela take the inhaler after? Second. How did Frank get it in the first place? *He* could have done it for all we know. Third – or is it fourth? – did Patel really bribe that copper? Fifth – why hasn't there been a memorial for Jameela?"

"That's obvious," I say. "She doesn't want anyone to know things aren't normal."

"That's what I mean, though. She should be trying to pretend everything is normal. But surely it would be *more* normal for her to have some kind of event, like for Morgan?"

"I really don't know," I admit. I put my face in my hands. "Ugh, it's all too much effort. Today has been a lot."

"Have you taken your meds?" Kat asks as she snuggles down.

"Yes, Mum." I smile. "Have you?"

She furrows a brow. "What do you mean?"

"Your shoulder. Or," I point at the offending area, "your lat or whatever it was. Feeling better?"

"Oh. Yeah, thanks." She looks uncomfortable and changes the subject. "You sleeping here again tonight, Tay?"

"Yeah." Her voice is muffled from behind the duvet. "If that's OK?"

"Of course it is," I say. "It's still your bed, even though you do have the fancy room upstairs."

The duvet shudders.

"I can't sleep up there. It was hard enough being up there on my own after Jameela, but since Friday, since Frank. . ."

"Hey, hey. I told you, it's still your bed, right, Kat?"

"Right," she agrees. That menthol smell drifts across the room as she discreetly rubs Tiger Balm into her shoulder.

"I'm gonna go brush my teeth." I stand and slide into flip-flops. The worn rubber is cool against my skin and I suppress a little shiver. "You coming, Tay?" She mumbles something unintelligible as I tug at the bottom of her cover.

"Yes, fine," she groans as she throws the duvet off and swaps it for a fluffy dressing gown.

We pad down the hallway to the shared bathroom, where our feet slap against the tiles. It's a cavern-like, stainless-steel room, the walls lined with squat, white porcelain tiles that cause echoes with every step. I'm glad Taylor is here — it's definitely not my favourite part of school to be alone in. We brush our teeth quickly, the silence between us secure, comfortable. I notice again how tired she looks – she really hasn't been sleeping. Second-year stress must be taking it out of her. I wonder if her face hurts.

We tiptoe back, aware of how quiet it is in the other dorms. I check my watch and realize it's almost an hour past lights out. Homework really does take longer this year; I mean, we all heard the seniors say that, but I just thought they were being dramatic.

We reach our dorm and gently close the door behind us. Kat is flaked out already, good sleep being a side effect of exercise or something ridiculous like that.

"Night, hon." Taylor gives me a hug and a kiss on the cheek, which I return, our nightly little routine. I never got a kiss before bedtime when I was growing up and my heart always swells a little, grateful that I found such a good friend.

"Night." I climb into bed and make myself comfortable, tucking my toes under the bottom of the duvet so the monsters don't get me, before reaching one arm out to switch off my lamp. Sleep doesn't come quickly to me in general, but no smartphone means no music, no reading fanfic under the covers and definitely no podcasts. Instead I let my eyes drift shut and do the deep-breathing exercises the doctor taught me. I place my hands on my stomach, breathing in through my nose until I feel my belly swell – then I let it out slowly, puffing my cheeks, expelling my breath through the small "O" of my mouth. I try it a few more times and allow my mind to drift back to the good things that came out of this weekend – namely Cole. Cole's fingers twining through my own as we walked around the lake, the way it felt to snuggle into the crook of his arm, however briefly that was. A sleepy smile twitches at the corners of my mouth as my mind unravels.

Until something scratches at the edges of my consciousness.

I can't quite put my finger on whatever it is, my mind half surrendered to sleep. Something someone said today, maybe? It's just out of my grasp, and I'm too far gone, so I have no choice but to relinquish it to oblivion.

Monday morning dawns way too early, but there's no chance of sleeping in when Kat is bouncing around your room. "Rise and shiiiine," she booms, yanking the duvet off me. My feet curl involuntarily as I crack one eye and see that she's already up and showered.

"Please tell me you haven't been to the gym already." I yawn, arching my back and stretching my arms out wide.

"Of course not." She grins. "Just a quick jog around the lake. You should come with me next time."

"Er, yeah. Maybe." I glance over at Taylor's empty bed, the duvet rumpled. "Where's Tay?" Taylor is normally harder to wake up than me.

"Dunno." Kat shrugs as she starts to comb through her wild brown hair. "She was already gone when I got back from my run. Come on, you better get up. I'm starving, going to head straight down."

"OK, OK." I grab my shower bag and pull a towel from the hamper. "Save me a seat, I won't be long." I walk back down to the bathroom, the sounds of hairdryers and morning chatter filtering through the doors. Like the night before, though, there's just one thing on my mind, only now I remember what it is.

How come Taylor couldn't sleep thinking about Frank on Friday, when she didn't find out until Saturday morning?

21

For people who are meant to be so intelligent, that inhaler wasn't hidden particularly well. I waited until the early morning, while they were still asleep, and searched the room on silent feet. And there it was, in a plastic bag, under the bed. I mean, come on.

UNDER THE BED.

I'll feel better once I get rid of it. Stupid, stupid Frank. He had to get himself involved, didn't he? Now they're all sniffing around like the bloody Scooby gang.

I really didn't think it would have to go this far. Now it's like I don't have a choice any more. The dice have been rolled for me.

If I want to succeed there will have to be more accidents. It's as simple as that.

22

The dining room is full when I arrive and back to normal after the lavish weekend, which means self-service cereal or fruit. I grab some cornflakes with a splash of oat milk – dairy really messes with my head these days – and an apple, then go to find the others.

"Hey." I slide on to the bench across from Marcus and Cole. Cole gives me a shy smile, which makes me feel warm inside. "Where are the others?"

"Gone already," Marcus says. "Kat has some early-doors study group in the library and Taylor was leaving when we got here." He shakes his head. "Girl is working way too hard."

"Yeah," I murmur, "but she's got a lot to live up to this year." Shouts and laughter echo around the dining hall and for a second, I can almost believe that everything is ... normal. "Right?"

"Yeah, she does." He stirs a spoon of sugar into his mug. "You see the picture of Frank in the hallway? Seems Patel wants some kind of a memorial this time."

"Yeah." I spotted it coming down the stairs. The same easel that Morgan's photo had been propped up on, the same black fabric skimming the floor. "I still can't believe it. I know Frank could be intense, but he was pretty funny sometimes too, you know. And that boy knew his ancient civilizations."

"Yeah, I did a bit of head/deputy stuff with him last week, before he ... well, you know." Marcus clears his throat as Cole and I exchange glances. "Anyway, I'd better shoot, too." Marcus stands up and points at us both in turn. "Let you two catch up." He wiggles his eyebrows to break the tension and grabs his tray, dropping it back at the hatch before striding out the door.

"Smooth," Cole laughs.

"Cringe," I agree.

I lift a jug from the table and pour it into a glass, tiny ghosts of ice cubes flowing out with the water. I reach into my pocket for my tablets and hesitate – do I want Cole to see me take these? Well, it's that or take them later without food and that makes me feel queasy. I don't want to feel like I did the last time that happened. I pull out the blister packet and pop two pills from the silver foil, drop them into my mouth and wash them down with a swig of water. Cole doesn't bat an eyelid. I think he's actually perfect.

"You got a class first thing?" he asks as he wipes his hands on a linen napkin. No paper here – it might be a standard breakfast on a weekday, but it's still Morton.

"I do." I check my watch. "Not until nine, though, so I've got half an hour. You?"

"Same," he says, leaning back in his chair and stretching long arms over his head. His white shirt is crisp and starched and just the tiniest bit too tight. His top button is undone, allowing a glimpse of his neck.

He says something and I have to shake myself to attention.

"Sorry, what?"

Cole gives me a grin that turns my stomach inside out. "I said, do you want to go for a walk?"

"I have a better idea." I place the uneaten apple into my bag for later, throw the strap over one shoulder and climb back over the bench. My tartan skirt rides up and I'm sure I catch him looking. "You wanna see the secret way upstairs?"

"The secret way?" He stands too and shrugs on his blazer, which looks twice the size of mine. The pop of acid green piping does something wonderful to his eyes.

"Yeah." We both lift our trays and head back to the serving hatch, sliding them on to waiting trolleys. "It's the old servants' stairs, from when this was a manor house. You know, so that the rich people wouldn't see the servants coming and going. We're not really supposed to use them but everyone does."

We head out and stop in front of a solid wooden door. "Storeroom?" Cole asks.

"Yep." I glance around furtively and grab the handle. "Come on." We slip inside and close the door behind us. I fumble for the light switch, flipping the old-fashioned lever. Ancient fluorescent lights flicker and groan overhead as we walk through the large pantry. I see Cole eyeing a shelf of biscuits and catch his hand.

"Don't even think about it," I warn him. "The cook has, like, psychic abilities when it comes to stock levels. Marcus got done for nicking some Jaffa Cakes last year and I reckon he's still scared of her."

"Consider me warned. So where's this staircase?"

"Back here." I walk to the rear of the room and lay my hand on a door. It's nothing like the one we came in through, though it's just as old. The timber is splintered at the bottom, where it has caught on the stone step over the years, and the handle is just a piece of rope that has been looped through a roughly hewn hole in the wood. It's not a door meant for noble eyes. I pull the rope handle towards me and a cold draught hits us both as it swings out. I shiver. "No heating in there," I tell him. "No lights either, so be careful."

"OK." The door groans shut and we're plunged into darkness as Cole starts to climb the steps behind me. Something brushes my hand and I give a little yelp. "Sorry, it's just me." He grabs my hand, more firmly than he has so far, and I relish the heat that seeps from his skin as he joins me on the same step.

"I can't see anything. Maybe we should wait a minute, let our eyes adjust," he says, his voice low. I can just make out his shape in the darkness and feel as though I'm being drawn towards him. "Are you cold?"

"A little." My voice is low and husky too, and the roof of my mouth is suddenly desert-like. Cole takes a step closer and his body brushes against mine. I move back automatically, the cold stone of the wall pressing into my back, even though all I want to do is lean into him.

"Sorry," he whispers again.

"Don't be."

He takes another step forwards and then our bodies are pressing together and all I can feel is the heat of him. "Without sounding like a total creep, I've wanted to do this since the first time I saw you," he whispers as he slips his hands beneath my blazer and wraps them around my waist. I'm fairly sure I've stopped breathing and I can actually hear the blood pounding around my body. I mirror him automatically, my arms sliding beneath the

146

scratchy grey tweed of his jacket. My pulse quickens; he's so warm. My head lifts towards his of its own accord and his lips find mine in the darkness.

The kiss is slow at first – soft, hesitant, his lips pillowing my own – but gradually it becomes something deeper, more urgent, and our bodies are pressed into one another and his hands are wrapped in my hair and I don't even care about my scar and...

"Was that the bell?" Cole whispers the words between kisses on the base of my neck and it takes me a second to come round, remember where I am. He slides his hands back down to my waist and I take a deep, shaking breath.

"The ... the what?"

He laughs and drops another kiss on to my lips, which quickly turns into another.

"The five-minute bell," he repeats, resting his forehead against my own.

"What? No, you can't be serious!" He releases me and my whole body feels in danger of collapse as I try to focus. "Ugh, we need to go, now." I pick up my bag from the floor, even though I have precisely no recollection of how it got there, and start to take the steps two at a time. A sliver of light comes into view as we reach the second floor and I push open a door that's the twin of the one downstairs. We emerge into a small cleaning closet, stacked with mops and sprays and stinking of bleach. I go to open the next door when he pulls me back.

"Wait." His grin is crooked, mischievous, as he whirls me around. For a second I think he's going to kiss me again and, you know what, it won't make a difference if I'm late for one class and... "Here." He runs his hands over my hair and I realize that if I look as dishevelled as he does, I might as well be wearing a shirt emblazoned with "just in from an early-morning make-out sesh" on it.

His hands fix my collar and I return the favour, neatening the knot of his tie and smoothing his hair back into place where I must have smooshed it with overeager hands.

"Better?" I ask.

"Perfect," he replies, leaning down for one more kiss. It's soft and lingering and over way too soon. We give ourselves one final shake and emerge to see people filtering into classrooms. There are more than a few raised eyebrows and I *should* be embarrassed but we just grin at each other. I kind of wish I had that T-shirt now.

"See you at lunch?"

"Definitely." He squeezes my hand before heading in the direction of the science lab and I practically float to my classics lesson. I'm feeling disgustingly happy when I'm brought back to earth with a bump.

"Well?" Emily stands sentry in front of the classroom, arms folded. She looks awful. The smile slides from my face.

"Not here," I whisper, trying to sound reassuring.

"There are teachers around. We can talk later, after JB tonight."

"Fine." She steps aside, leaving the doorway clear so I can pass. "But I'm holding you to it."

23

As it turns out, I don't see Cole at lunch. After classics, with its two empty desks and Emily glaring at the back of my head all morning, I have the worst headache coming on. I head back to the dorm for some painkillers – even though what I actually want to do is climb into bed and cry for three hours straight. What was I doing, thinking I could be happy, when everything is so scary and confusing?

The corridor is empty – we're not really supposed to come back until later – and kind of spooky, but if I don't address this now I'll just be really sick this afternoon.

I unlock the door to our room only to be confronted by a figure sitting at our dressing table.

"Taylor! What are you doing up here?"

"I could ask you the same question." She turns around on the stool so I can see the concealer stick in her hand. "I'm trying to cover up this." She gestures to the raised area of skin on her cheek. I frown and come closer. It looks much worse than it did last night.

"Is that from the other night?"

"Yeah, the stupid loose nail in my blusher brush. Cheap market tat. It seemed to be fine but today it's just. . ." She stops and makes an exploding motion with her free hand.

"Ugh, I'm sorry. It looks sore. Here." I head to my bedside table and pull open the drawer, or the medicine cabinet, as we call it – I'm the one with all of the paracetamol, the ointments and plasters. "Put some of this on it."

"Thanks." Taylor takes the little tub of antibacterial ointment and smears some directly on to the scratch, dabbing it in with a pinkie finger. "What are you doing up here, anyway?"

"Headache." I grimace, holding up a packet of ibuprofen. Should I tell her about Emily? I watch as she dabs concealer on to the scratch and I swallow hard. "Er, Tay? Can I ask you something?"

"Sure." She doesn't turn to face me but her eyes watch me through the mirror. "What is it?"

"I was just wondering, I mean, I wanted to ask you . . . you said something last night that. . ." The words spill out over on top of one another and I pause to gather them back together into a more coherent sentence. "Last night you said you couldn't sleep alone on Friday because of Frank. But you couldn't have known he was dead on Friday – you were already asleep when we got back – so how did you know?"

"Oh, God, is that all?" She dabs blusher on to the apples of her cheeks and I admire how deftly she hides the scratch. "I thought you were going to ask me to move out of the dorm or something! I know it's not really fair that I have the head girl room and never use it. . ."

"No, of course not! I was just wondering how, well, how you knew. That's all."

She doesn't answer for a minute, concentrating on her make-up. "Marcus told me," she says at last.

I take a breath. "But you wouldn't have seen Marcus," I said.

"Well, he texted me on my burner. Said Frank had been found in the woods. It gave me the creeps."

"Oh." I guess that makes sense. So why do I feel so uneasy?

"What?" She turns to face me now and there's a glimmer of something – anger? – in her eyes. "Don't you believe me?"

"Jeez, Tay, of course I do! But I'm freaking out here – first Morgan, then Jameela, Frank. . . That inhaler had something in it that should NOT have been there and I . . .

152

I . . ." My breath is coming in hiccupping gulps now and tears burn the inner corner of my eyes. I try my best to push it back and take deep breaths, let my mind go blank, block everything out. I don't want to have a fight, not now.

"Hey, hey." There's a warm hand on my back as the bed dips beside me, taking Taylor's weight. "Deep breaths. I know, it's insane, I don't know what's going on but . . . wait." She stops dead. "*Morgan*? You actually think Morgan was murdered?"

"No. Yes. Oh, I don't know!" My breathing is still shaky and I suck in some shallow gulps of air. "But remember the note? '*Morgan's death was not an accident. I killed her. And you're next.*' That's what it said. Jameela read it out last Monday at the meeting and the next thing we know, she's dead. Frank thought there was something wrong with her inhaler and he's found dead. Are you telling me this didn't start with Morgan?"

There's a silence. All I can hear is my own ragged breathing.

"You're saying that Jameela and Frank were killed because they got involved," says Taylor slowly.

I nod. "Yeah. I think they were asking too many questions, just like. . ."

"Just like us," Taylor finishes. Her eyes meet mine, wide and scared. "Oh God."

"Yep," I agree.

"Right." She hops to her feet and checks her watch.

"We haven't had this conversation. I want you to carry on playing dumb – well, you know, not *dumb*, but act like you don't know anything about what was found in the inhaler."

"Er, that might be a problem. Emily ambushed me today before classics."

Taylor holds up a hand. "Leave her to me. She's going to be sworn in as deputy head girl tonight, so she will have to listen to me, OK?"

"OK." If Taylor's right – if Emily has a trace of self-preservation, she'll keep her mouth shut tonight, at least until after we have spoken to her. Unfortunately, despite Morton being full of some of the most intelligent people I've ever met, common sense can be pretty thin on the ground.

"Come on, we'd better go." Taylor leans down to glance in the mirror one last time, pulls a brush through her hair and stands up straight. "What have you got this afternoon?"

"Art."

"Nice. Wish I could draw," she says, holding the door open for me, "but I am strictly a stick people kinda gal."

"Yeah, it's a nice class." We head down the corridor to the main staircase, but Taylor looks distracted.

"Hey, what's up?" I ask.

"Nothing." She carries on walking but I grab hold of her arm and we stop in the middle of the hallway. "Oh, I'm fine. I just keep thinking about something, that's all."

"What? Come on, you can tell me."

"I know, I guess I just don't want to say it out loud."
I wait, not saying anything, a trick I learned from my
doctor in hospital over the summer. Give her time and she
will talk, if she really wants to. "It's just . . . well, if what
you said about Morgan is right, if she was, you know . . .
killed . . . then you know what that means, don't you?"

I stay quiet as she gains the energy to voice her fears
aloud.

"It means one of us really *did* do it, as in someone from
Jewel and Bone. There was no one else there that night
on the lake; it was just us who took the boats out. . . That
ridiculous initiation, we should never have agreed to it . . .
then Patel and Creepy Billy were there and. . ." Her words
fade out as she carries on talking.

Another thought has taken hold, one that I can't ignore.

Taylor said that Marcus told her about Frank. But
Marcus wasn't with us when we found Frank. He was back
in his dorm, asleep.

So how the hell did he know what had happened?

Art class is always just what I need. It really does calm me down, especially with so much pressure on this year. When the lesson comes to an end, I linger behind, tidying up slowly, packing away pieces of charcoal and taking my time washing my hands in the large porcelain sink, the kind you see in old farmhouses. I watch the soot rinse from my fingers, grey swirls disappearing down the drain.

"Hey," a voice calls from the other side of the room and I turn to see Cole poking his head around the doorframe. "Taylor said I might find you here. Do you mind?"

"No, not at all!" I take a wedge of paper towels and dry my hands quickly, grabbing my portfolio and putting it away on to the rack. Cole does not need to see the inner workings of my brain, not yet anyway. "I'm sorry I didn't see you at lunch."

"Hey, don't worry." He's hovering in the doorway, hands jammed deep into his pockets now. "As long as you're not avoiding me, you know, after this morning?"

"No!" Oh God, I practically just shouted that right in his face. "No, sorry, I just had a headache." I join him at the door. "Emily was hounding me this morning."

"Oh. Yikes."

"Yeah." I don't want to go into too much detail, especially after slipping up and almost telling him about JB when I mentioned Old Josef the other day. Can you imagine his reaction if I told him I was part of a secret society that stands around the bones of a dead guy in velvet robes, all so a top university will consider me? I change the subject quickly. "What are you up to now?"

"Homework, or prep as you guys call it. Want to join me?"

"Actually, yeah, that sounds perfect. I have some modern history stuff I need to look up. Library?"

"Sounds like a plan. Can we stop for cake in the common room first, though? Marcus said you get afternoon tea every day now."

My stomach grumbles. "Of course," I reply, "I am always down for cake."

*

The common room is rammed, as usual – cake, scones and tea come out at four and by then everyone is ravenous after a day of lessons. I select a scone – no raisins, thank you very much – with butter, some of Creepy Billy's home-made jam which is, quite frankly, amazing, and a cup of steaming hot Earl Grey tea. We join the others in what I already think of as "our" seats and I notice that Cole's plateful of Victoria sponge is rivalled only by Marcus's. There's a happy, crumb-filled silence and when I've inhaled my scone, I curl up on to the seat, satiated by the sugar. The shallow, white cup is between my hands, and I relish the heat seeping into my bones. I miss mugs, though.

"You miss what?" Kat asks, between mouthfuls of lemon drizzle.

"Er, mugs." I really did need to watch what I was saying aloud – how embarrassing. Mugs. I cringe inwardly.

"I get it," Cole chimes in, delicately picking up his cup, the handle between his thumb and forefinger. "These things have like a thimbleful of tea in them. Give me a chipped mug with a builder's brew in it any day."

"Agreed!" I laugh. I do like the Earl Grey better but he doesn't have to know that. "So, what's everyone doing before dinner?"

A chorus of "prep" goes up and Cole gives me a wry smile. Looks like we'll have company. We return our plates to the trolley and wander over to the library, the five of us talking quietly as we enter. The desk by my Bernini is empty and I make a beeline towards it, drop my bag as the others settle on the benches and head straight over to the circular central desk where the computers are.

"How does this thing work, then, if there's no internet?" I swear I feel the whisper of a kiss on the back of my neck as Cole appears behind me and I almost full-on swoon.

"Oh, there is internet, just not on these. You need to book internet time on one of the laptops, so it can be monitored. This is easy, though, you just type in your class and there's usually a list of recommended reading, like this." I point to the screen where my modern history reading list is displayed. "I have a paper due on small-town legends. So I click here." I press the screen and a title is highlighted by a blue bar. I repeat the process. "Then here and here," two more blue bars, "then hit submit."

The small printer whirrs and spits out a square piece of paper. On top is my name, the date and time and the list of books I've requested.

"Then we take it to the librarian. She's really good; she can usually recommend a couple of extras that aren't on the list, if you tell her what you're doing." I point at the screen. "Your turn."

When both of us have paper slips we follow the curve of the desk around to the opposite side, where Ms Somerville, the librarian, is stacking books on to a trolley.

"Liz, how lovely to see you! And Cole, is it? You're the new student." It's more of a statement than a question – Ms Somerville knows everyone – and she quickly moves on. "What can I get you today?"

We place our slips on to the highly polished wooden desk and she studies them. "Chemistry, botanics, very good. Actually, I know an excellent book that looks at the chemistry of plants; it will link these topics up for you. I'll bring it out. And Liz, urban legends, now that is interesting. I have some original sources in the archives; I think you'll enjoy them."

"Thank you." She lifts the counter and bustles off to the shelves, deftly selecting books. "Come on, she'll bring them over."

He follows me back to the desk. "OK, so urban legends? That's pretty cool."

"Yeah, I love how something gets so twisted by retellings. This essay I'm doing is choosing one and unpicking it, laying out the facts and trying to identify the historical basis – there usually is at least one. Everywhere has their own urban legends, if you ask around. I'm surprised there aren't more about Morton, to be honest."

"I bet there are some," he says enthusiastically. "We just have to ask the right people."

"True. I've only heard the usual – saying Bloody Mary into the mirror on the second-floor loos, the white lady in the woods, that sort of stuff."

"Ever done it? The Bloody Mary thing?"

"God, no. I'm not stupid, Cole." I bump him with my

hip as he follows me back to the table and we sit, smiling at each other. I wonder if he's been constantly reliving this morning, too. Kat is already hidden behind a graphic novel of *The Tempest* and Taylor and Marcus have their heads bowed together over a very detailed drawing of the human anatomy. Cole raises his eyebrows and I stifle a giggle.

"Here we go." Ms Somerville appears as if by magic and Taylor slams the cover of her manuscript shut. Ms Somerville just smiles and deposits a pile of books in front of Cole before placing a mixture of books and brown envelopes on my desk. "Now, Liz, these are originals, so please take great care with them. Put them back into the envelopes when you are finished."

"I will, thanks Ms Somerville." I pick up the topmost envelope. There are two small circles on the flap and they have a short length of string wrapped around them in a figure of eight, keeping the envelope sealed. I carefully unravel it and slide open the pamphlet inside.

It doesn't look too old, maybe the 1990s or so. It's a brochure for some kind of spooky walking tour, at a place called Gallow Ford. I read through the legends and put it to one side, thinking it might be useful later, and open the second envelope.

This one is more local and I recognize some of the stories from the ones the seniors tried to frighten us with last year. I skim through the small booklet and note down any tales I haven't heard of, before stopping on one particular page.

"Hey, guys," I whisper. Four pairs of eyes swivel in my direction. "Look at this."

I spin the booklet around and point at the short article entitled "*Club or Cult?*"

"Have you guys ever heard of this? A cult from around here in the late nineties?"

"A cult?" Kat's eyes sparkle with undisguised morbid glee. She loves this sort of thing. "Oooh, I listened to so many podcasts about cults this summer! But no, I didn't know there was one around here." She pauses to skim-read the article, occasionally shaking her head as we all stare at her, our resident murderino. "OK, this is grim."

"Why grim?" Marcus asks, half listening and half taking notes for his homework.

"Because they killed people. This guy – Bradley Harrison – he convinced his followers to murder others. Like Charles Manson." Kat looks up to a pool of blank faces. "Oh, you're kidding! You've never heard of Charlie Manson?"

"Nooooo," Taylor says as we shake our heads.

"Ridiculous. OK – so Manson had a cult in the sixties. His followers committed a bunch of murders because he told them to and he didn't lift a finger." She taps the article. "Sounds like this guy did the same thing in the nineties. Got his followers to kill on his behalf."

"Jeez," Taylor whispers. "And it wasn't that long ago?"

"Well, before we were born," I explain.

"Ugh, that's awful," murmurs Taylor "And around here? The nearest town is Prescott and that's tiny! I wonder where this stuff happened?"

"Kind of all over. Looks like he had links to Prescott, or close by anyway, but some of the murders were in Oxford, Boston, London. . ." I trail off as I read the others. Cambridge, New York.

"University towns?" Cole reads my thoughts.

"Yeah, I guess. They had a pretty huge reach for a cult, though. That's scary. He must have been transatlantic."

"Does it say how they died?" Kat asks, her eyes on the page.

"Here, take it." I push the article over to her and Kat starts to read out loud. For some reason my heart has started beating hard.

"Drowning," she says. "Poisoning. . ."

"And let me guess," Cole interrupts, "being beaten with a rock?"

Kat looks up. "Amongst other things, yes."

My mind spins until all I can see is the blur of faces around me. My brain is working overtime.

"Wait, so how did the leader" – I lean over and consult the article – "this Bradley Harrison – get his followers to *kill* people for him?" I ask, taking the paper back and reading to the end so I can answer my own question.

"Cult leaders are meant to be very charismatic," Kat says. "And it sounds like he promised them success, financial security, all that stuff."

I shudder. "Who would want to do something like that?"

Kat's eyes are shining. "The 'Transcendental Faithful' by the looks of it. I mean, he would have been totally sociopathic, had no empathy for others. He just wanted to get to the top of the pile and everyone else be damned. He just got other people to do his dirty work for him." She is silent, biting her lip. "Wait. Are we saying. . ."

"Spit it out," Taylor laughs, but her voice is quiet. Nervous.

We all know what Kat's going to say.

"Are they . . . back? The cult? What if that explains what has been going on. This is the perfect spot for a cult to take root and commit a load of murders." She prods the paper with a bitten fingernail. "I mean, look around."

"At what?" Marcus says, trying for a joke. "We're totally isolated."

"Exactly. The school is secluded," I murmur in agreement. "The closest bus stop is a twenty-minute walk away and then it's another forty-five minutes to get into Prescott, if you're lucky. Which means. . ."

"Which means we're sitting ducks," Kat says.

25

The smoky smell of melting wax burrows into my nose as I follow Taylor down the steps in the old chapel. I shrug on the velvet cape, just as I did a week earlier, our Monday ritual. So much has happened since.

"You think Patel will initiate more acolytes? You know, to replace Jameela and Frank?" I hiss to Taylor, as she tucks her red hair beneath her hood.

"I dunno." Her voice is so low I have to strain to hear. "They didn't replace Morgan, did they? Even though they had all summer. I reckon we'll be getting ready to start meeting and greeting Jewel and Bone donors, soon, looking for sponsors. But who knows?"

We follow the procession of silent, black-clad figures that glide around the circle, over the stagnant water. It has been a warm week and the smell is unmistakable but bearable. Just.

Dr Patel starts her intonation and invites the new head girl up to the centre. I watch it all like it's happening to someone else – watch as Taylor goes through the motions, watch as Emily is called up to take the place of deputy head. For the first time at one of these meetings, my mind begins to drift – it's hard to think that a week ago I was bursting with excitement. I wonder if I'll ever get that feeling back.

I peer out to the side from beneath my hood and count the figures standing around me. Four empty plinths. I start a tick list in my head: Taylor and Emily, that's two; Morgan and Jameela makes four. But there's no empty place where Frank should be. Have they filled the spot? A new deputy head boy?

Interesting.

I look back in time to see Taylor and Emily lay their bloodied hands on Old Josef. I recite the words with the others.

"Excellent. I sincerely hope that this is the final time we must initiate a new head girl this academic year." Patel's voice is cold and businesslike. "However, before we come to our usual business, we must induct one new member. Acolyte, please approach."

I was right. There's a murmur from a few of the members who must not have noticed the extra body in the room. A figure breaks away from its podium and strides forward confidently, ripples of velvet drifting in its wake. Whoever it is tall, taller than me because the tail ends of their cloak don't drag through the water beneath, like mine tend to do. They reach the centre and Patel instructs them to remove their hood.

They do.

"Cole," I breathe.

My heart tightens a little. Yes, there's a sliver of relief, I guess, that I can talk to him about this stuff now, stop hiding it from him, but it's overshadowed by anxiety. Will he stop whatever is going on between us because I didn't tell him about this? Will he think I'm a liar, trust me less?

He is initiated into the fold in a blur and before I know it, hoods are removed and a round of applause goes up to welcome our newest member. I join in and smile when he catches my eye, but, in the pit of my stomach, I feel something like dread.

"Here he is!"

Cole appears at the glass balcony doors of the girls' senior lounge and Marcus jumps to his feet, whooping and cheering. Cole smiles back but there's a red flush to his cheeks as he enters. The room is empty, apart from us.

The weather is balmy and beautiful for a September

evening, but since Jameela's death last week, no one has ventured outside to the roof garden, or up here at all really, unless it's to leave cards, candles or bunches of wildflowers. The latter are decaying now, their petals turning to brown mulch, but no one has moved them.

"Hey." Cole joins us quietly and slides into the empty seat next to me. He smiles. "So, I really am part of the gang now, right?"

"I'm sorry we didn't tell you," I say, and the others murmur in half-hearted agreement, "but, you know, secret society and all that."

"Yeah, I get it." He stares off into the distance.

"So," Marcus interrupts loudly, "how does it feel to have almost beaten my time in the hunt?"

Cole scratches the back of his head and grins, this shy smile that's the most endearing thing I've ever seen. "It feels good. Though I'll tell you what, when I got that note stabbed on to my pillow with a skull badge, inviting me to 'The Hunt' I wondered what the hell I'd got myself into."

"It seems scary," I reassure him, "but it's just a good old scavenger hunt. You must have made good time on it to take the deputy place, though?'

"Yeah. In fact, you helped with that."

"I did? How?"

"When you showed me around the library, remember when you showed me that poison Bible?" I nod. The others have stopped paying attention. Marcus and Taylor start to whisper and Kat starts texting, grinning down at the little screen on her burner phone. I take advantage of the fact and lean in even closer to Cole. "Well, when I got to the last riddle, the one about a *holy disguise*, I went to look at it again. It's right by that massive window, the one with the picture of a chapel in it. When the sun shone on it. . ."

". . .it practically pointed the way," I finish for him.

"Yeah," he grins, before touching a kiss to the tip of my nose. "So, thank you."

"You are so welcome." How long is acceptable to stare into someone's eyes at such close range? I can't tear my gaze away from him. I let out a deep sigh, not realizing the others can hear me. The cackle of our friends bursting into laughter kind of breaks the spell. I pull myself away from Cole a little.

"Well," Kat says loudly, breaking the awkward silence as she rearranges herself on her armchair, folding her legs beneath her and pulling her long sleeves down over her hands. "If the lovebirds have quite finished, we have more important stuff to attend to. Who wants to know what I found out today?"

"How gruesome is it?" asks Taylor. "I'm gonna need to know if it's gross or not first." She's curled up with Marcus on a cuddle chair, her legs stretched over his lap as he lazily draws circles on her bare knees. Taylor touches her cheek gingerly, a raised line now visible beneath her make-up. "I don't know if I can take more murder cult stuff."

"Nothing gruesome. Well, not really." Kat leans forwards. "It's about Creepy Billy."

"Creepy Billy? Wait." Cole looks at me. "That's the groundskeeper you told me about, right?"

"Right."

"Yep. So," Kat continues, "I saw him just before we left for JB tonight, wheeling that ancient little barrow of his around. Seriously, as if Morton won't get him a new one, it's basically an antique. Anyway, I saw him talking to a student. . ." She trails off dramatically.

"Right," I prompt her, "what's so weird about that?"

"Well." Kat pauses, enjoying our undivided attention. "*Said student* handed him something and Billy handed something back. Something wrapped in brown paper."

"Someone was buying off him?" Marcus asks.

"*Buying off him?*" Kat snorts. "What are you, some kind of drug lord?"

Marcus's jaw tightens. "I saw a thing or two growing up."

Taylor strokes his cheek and diverts Kat's attention. "What was in the brown paper?" she asks.

"I dunno." Kat shrugs. "But who knows what he grows out there on his allotment. It could have been anything."

"You think it was *drugs*, then?" I whisper the word, even though we're the only ones up here. "You think he's growing something and selling it to students? That's a serious accusation to make."

"That's what it looked like." Kat holds her hands palm up. "Just saying it like I saw it. There is one really important question you have failed to ask me, though."

"I was just about to." Taylor yawns. "Sorry about that. So, Kat, just who did you see meeting with our very own creepy groundskeeper in such a nefarious manner?"

Kat leans back in her seat, eyes twinkling as she answers. "Emily."

There had been much discussion about *exactly* what Emily had been buying from Creepy Billy before we sloped off to bed last night. Now, in the bright light of a Tuesday morning, it's as clear as mud.

I get dressed slowly this morning. Outside, the sun is shining and the leaves are beginning to turn. Taylor and Kat are already gone. I head out into the corridor, looking cautiously around – I don't want to run into Emily on my own. I decide I'll run down to the dining hall for an apple and then go the secret way to class. My lips twitch in a smile as I think about what happened when I went that way to class yesterday. . .

"Liz." Emily emerges from the shadows by her dorm room and I curse inwardly.

"Hey, Emily." I make a show of looking at my battered leather wristwatch and yawning. "Can't stop, I slept in and class starts in ten minutes, so. . ."

"Don't give me that." Her voice is cold, monotone and the hairs on the back of my neck stand up. For a person who usually looks so perfectly groomed, she couldn't look much worse. There are dark circles under her eyes and her skin is washed out, pasty looking. Her hair is down but in need of a wash, grease parting the roots. She looks like the poster girl for smoking things you shouldn't. I wonder if Creepy Billy really is dealing stuff on the side? "I've been waiting to talk to you."

"Now?"

"Yes, *now*. Why are you all avoiding me?" Emily's dull eyes bore into mine and I'm suddenly hyper aware that we're alone. No one would hear us up here if anything happened.

"I'm not," I say weakly. "*We're* not. We're all just . . . busy."

"Seriously?" Emily tucks dull locks behind her ears and her eyelid flickers in a twitch I haven't noticed before. "That's all you can come up with? I ask you to help me find out who killed my best friend and you're *busy*?"

"Emily, listen. I'm sorry, I really am. But you know that we will get in so much trouble if we're late for class and—" She holds up a dismissive hand to cut me off.

"Liz, I just want you to help me. Something weird is going on and I'm ... I'm running out of people I can trust." Her face crumples and for the first time, I see below her cold exterior. "I can't sleep, Ayesha is useless and my other friends are d ... d ... dead." The last word comes out in huge, hiccupping gulps and I can see she's on the verge of a panic attack.

"OK, OK." I gently grab hold of her forearms and look her in the eye as sobs wrack her chest. "I'll help you, of course I will." I glance at the watch on my outstretched arm and nod to it. "But look, we really will be late for class. I don't know about you, but I don't want to be on a report card right at the start of the year, do you?"

"Fine." She pulls away and, just like that, her stony expression returns. "I'll be at the library later, for prep. Make sure you come and find me. There's something I want to show you."

"OK." I breathe a sigh of relief. "Of course, I'll be there."

"I mean it, Liz." She starts to walk away but hesitates. Emily turns back on her heel and points a shaking finger at me. "I'm deputy head girl now. Make sure you're there or your first Jewel and Bone sponsor meeting won't happen. Understand?" She storms off then, leaving my words trailing behind her as she stalks down the corridor

I guess I don't have a choice.

*

The rest of Tuesday passes in a blur of lessons. At the end of the day, I catch sight of Kat on the balcony that rings the central staircase. I sharpen my elbows and push through the throng until I get to her. "Hey, Kat!"

"Liz!" She pauses, waiting for me to catch up and I feel the little thrill I often get from being up so high. It's some drop from here to the bottom of the stairs. "Good day?"

"Not bad." I fall into step with her and we follow the crowd down the stone steps. "Need to talk to you guys, though."

"Oh? About you-know-who?"

"Yeah, not here, though." We traipse to the bottom in silence.

She nods, once. "OK, tell you what. Let's grab the others — and some cake — and discuss." I nod in relieved agreement.

The late afternoon sun follows us down the corridor as we pass the library on our way to the common room. I make myself as small as possible, in case Emily is already in there, ready to pounce.

Our table is empty, so I sink gratefully into the cool leather and close my eyes. Kat heads to the tea table as I mentally run through that day's prep — carry on researching that local history essay, start some still life studies for a new art project and pull together a presentation on the French Revolution. Unfortunately, none of it is as interesting as what I *really* want to look up — that local cult.

"Hey honey." I prise open tired eyes as Taylor and Marcus flop on to the sofa across the table. "Good day?"

"Not bad," I repeat. I study Taylor's cheek – it seems to be a bit more swollen today, more visible beneath her make-up. Maybe I should tell her to get it looked at, but I don't want to freak her out even more right now. For someone who wants to be a doctor, she's got a weird thing about needles. "You?"

Taylor shrugs. "Same. Busy."

We sit in comfortable silence as Kat approaches with a plateful of goodies and a cup of Earl Grey for me. "Thank you." I take the tiny white cup and blow across the rim, watching the steam float away, the string from the teabag dancing. I grab the tab and swirl it around before lifting it out and placing it on to the matching saucer, where the liquid pools. "Listen, I need to talk to you guys, but I want to wait till Cole gets here. Where is he, anyway? Didn't you guys have a class with him last thing?"

"Yeah." Marcus sprays crumbs and Taylor squeals and slaps his thigh. "Sorry." He swallows and grins at us. "He went back to his room for something, said he'd meet us here," Marcus says.

"Oh, OK." I settle back and take a tiny sip of tea. I yelp – it's *way* too hot. "Shit!" I put the cup down, my tongue on fire.

"Lizzie! Wash your mouth out!" Kat is laughing incredulously, her face stretched in overexaggerated shock.

"What do you mean?"

"You, swearing! I don't think I've ever heard a naughty word from your mouth before. You've changed."

"It was hot," I say innocently. She chuckles and I shrug, instead turning my attention to whether I want a chocolate-chip cookie or a scone when just then Cole appears, breathing hard.

"Hey." He drops down next to me and plants a kiss on my cheek like it's the most natural thing in the world. I avoid the ridiculous grins and Kat's shaking head and focus on Cole instead.

"Hi. Everything OK?"

"Yep. Just had to go and grab something." He reaches into his bag and rummages for a second. "Close your eyes."

"I – what?"

"Close your eyes," he repeats. I hesitate, but he looks so earnest I can't help but oblige. I sigh and squeeze my lids shut.

"Fine. But if you play any kind of trick on me..."

"As if I would. Now, hold out your hands."

"Oh, come on, Cole, I don't like surprises."

"Trust me," he says, taking hold of my hands and placing them face up on my lap. My mind flashes to all the things he could put in there – something gross, a spider or a bug... "Ready?"

I nod hesitantly.

"OK," he says and I feel the weight of a cool, smooth

object in my hands. It feels familiar and as I wrap a hand around it, I feel the handle and a "C" carved into the side. I open my eyes and stare at it.

"It's a mug," Cole explains.

"A mug?" I repeat stupidly as Taylor squeals across the table.

"Yeah, you know, the other day, you said you missed mugs. And I had this one that my mum gave me, but I don't really drink tea, so..." He trails off. "I'm sorry, It's stupid, isn't it?"

"No!" I twirl the mug in my hands and smile up at him. "It's so thoughtful to bring it down."

"Really?"

"Really." I lean forwards and kiss him softly on the lips. "Thanks for letting me borrow it."

"Oh, no, it's yours." He smiles. "I want you to keep it. Like, a present. Is that OK?"

"Oh my GOD," Kat bellows over, "you two are ADORABLE. It's quite disgusting."

I grin down at the mug and back up at Cole. "Completely disgusting," I agree happily.

"We'll grab a table and keep an eye out for Emily and you guys go and see what you can find." Taylor steers Marcus and Cole across the library to an empty seat as Kat and I head to the computers. No one seemed particularly surprised that Emily had ambushed me this morning and we've agreed to tell her what we found out about the inhaler. But we also need to find out more about this cult.

"We want anything from late 1999 to early 2000, right?" Kat drops her bag on the floor next to mine as we start to navigate the system.

"Yeah, but where do we start? There's not exactly a section on 'murder cults', is there?" I notice a tall wooden cabinet in front of the far wall, between two windows. It's crammed full of tiny wooden drawers and I recognize it from my old school's library, where they hadn't fully computerized everything. "Look – there's a card catalogue. If that's organized by date, it could be easier to search?"

"OK." Kat collects both of our bags. I'm already five steps ahead of her. The closer we get to the card catalogue, the more the anticipation in my stomach builds. I have a good feeling about this.

That lasts for about three seconds.

"Well, they're not in date order," I say. The little drawers are arranged alphabetically, of course, and the small, typed labels all blur into one. Besides, my stomach hurts. I must have eaten too much cake earlier.

"No," Kat agrees, "but at least they're arranged by subject. Hmmmm." She starts to trail a finger along some drawers to the left. "A, B, C..."

"I doubt there's a section on cults, Kat." I sigh. My hand lowers to the waistband of my skirt and I tug at it a little, feeling suddenly bloated.

"Don't know if you don't try," she responds. "Wait, are you all right?"

A wave of cramps seizes me and I double over. It passes and I wave Kat off. "Ooof, just cramps. My period must be due. Come on, let's keep looking."

I'm right, though; there is nothing on cults. I try the "s" section as I rub my stomach. Nothing on secret societies, either.

"What about newspapers?" I say at last. "That article we saw was a clipping, wasn't it?"

"Yeah, a photocopy I think. But you're right, there must be old papers or something in the archives?"

"There's no drawer labelled 'newspapers'," I muse, the cogs in my brain not feeling particularly well-oiled today. God, my stomach hurts. "Do we know the names of any local papers? I have literally never seen one."

"The clipping was from the local paper – the *Prescott Times*, I think. Anything like that?"

I scour the drawers. "Yes," I gasp, drawing glances from people actually trying to study, and lower my voice. "Whoops. But yes, look." I tug at a small brass handle and the wooden drawer releases with a groan. "Eugh, it's so stiff! Here." I remove the first card, a plain rectangle, slightly yellowed with age. On it is typed some kind of code. "NC-03-12-99. Any ideas?"

Kat thinks for a moment. "NC – newspaper clipping? Newspaper cutting?"

"Ooh, good, yes, you genius. What about the rest? A date?"

"Possibly." Kat reads it again as I fight down another wave of cramps. I glance around and surreptitiously undo the button on the back of my skirt. Aah, that's better. "The third of the twelfth – so that's the third of December – 1999?"

"That sounds more like it." I flick through the next few cards and the dates start to go backwards rather than forwards. "They just get older – 99, 98, 97. Is there another drawer?" I push this one shut and look at the one beneath.

"Doesn't seem like it."

"Great." This was turning out to be a waste of time. "Why would they stop there? I mean, why remove anything more recent than the end of the last millennium?"

"I dunno." Kat's attention is waning. "Everything after 2000 might be in the digital archive. Listen, if it's not here, maybe we should leave it for now. I have so much prep to do and it's been so hard to concentrate recently. . ."

"I guess." It doesn't sit right with me, though – why just stop collecting newspapers after 1999? It seems like a very un-library thing to do. "I'm going to ask the librarian. Maybe they're somewhere else. You go and get on with whatever it is you need to do while you're in the mood. I know it's been hard to focus the last few days."

"Thanks, hon. Meet you back at the table."

"Sure." I make sure the drawer is shut properly and head

over to the central desk, where Ms Somerville is tidying away large folios on to a trolley, presumably to put back into storage.

"Hello again, Liz. Just a second." She hefts one more book on to the pile and turns to face me, her hand already outstretched for a ticket. "What will it be today?"

"I don't have a slip," I explain, holding my empty hands up. "I was hoping you could tell me if we have any newspaper clippings in the archives?"

"Of course we do." She points over to the card catalogue we have just been at. "You'll find most in there, though there are a few on the system. Most newspapers are automatically archived these days, though. Is it something in particular, dear?"

"Erm, yes, kind of. Do you remember the book you gave me yesterday, with all the local clippings in?"

"I do." Her expression is unreadable.

"There was something in there I'd like to know more about," I say, "for an essay."

"And what was that?"

"The, er, cult. The murder one."

"Oh, yes, the 'Transcendent Faithful', they called themselves." She lowers her voice and winces. "Oh, dear, no, I'm afraid you won't find anything else about that in here. It was a terribly messy affair. In fact, I'm surprised it's still in that book at all – shows how long it's been since somebody reserved that, I suppose."

"Why won't I be able to find out any more?"

"The records were removed, I'm afraid. When Morton employed a certain new headteacher, there was somewhat of a cull on the more . . . unsavoury aspects of the library. Unsavoury in Dr Patel's eyes, at least."

"I see," I mumble but inside I'm fizzing. How dare she! How dare Dr Patel get rid of information, like she's running some sort of fascist state rather than a school.

"Although." Ms Somerville glances around and lowers her voice. "I have heard tell that someone" – she tips her head towards the window and I follow it to see she's gesturing over at the allotment area – "has created their own kind of, clandestine, archive."

"Really? Creepy Billy, er, Mr Loomis?"

Ms Somerville straightens up. "I'm not sure I know what you mean," she responds, though her eyes are twinkling and she nods ever so slightly. "Now, can I get you anything else?"

27

"Why would Patel remove articles about that cult in particular, though?" Taylor mutters, eyes on a complicated-looking molecular diagram. "Unless she had something to do with it?"

"Nah," Marcus chimes in, his brow furrowed. "I mean, yeah, she can be a stone cold beeyatch, but that doesn't mean she was involved in some kind of murder cult. Or does it?"

"No," Kat says firmly, "it doesn't." She rolls her eyes. "I swear, it's the twenty-first century and if a woman still doesn't smile and make pretty for the men, she must have something wrong with her."

"Hey!" Marcus points the rubber end of his pencil at Kat. "I did not say that."

"But what if she *was* involved?" I ask, trying to connect the dots. "What if she was part of that cult all those years ago and now she's doing the same thing? Killing off students for some kind of power, control..."

"She already has that as headmistress," Kat argues. "We do whatever she says. Especially as acolytes – she's the one who will match us with donors who might turn into sponsors. She can make or break us."

There's a mumble of agreement around the table.

"What if she wanted more?" Cole says slowly. "What if she wants to be more than a headteacher?"

"That's a good point," says Taylor. "She was head girl at Morton when she was here. She would have had the pick of any college, any career she wanted. Do you think she loved Morton so much she wanted to come back and run the place?"

"Maybe." Kat taps a pen against her chin. "I mean, *we* do, don't we? Love it here, I mean."

"I do love it," Marcus says, "but I can't wait to see what else is out there, you know? And no offence to teachers, but I know I'm getting a full ride to study science at MIT – there's no chance I want to come back here as anything other than a future sponsor, to help some other kid out."

"Agreed," Taylor says. "I'm working too hard to let all

this go. We might have sponsorship but if you don't get the grades, you don't get the support."

Cole looks at me and voices what we're all thinking. "So what happened to Patel?"

"This is why we need to find out about this cult," says Kat.

I clear my throat. "I'm just going to ask him. Creepy Billy."

Cole levels a serious look across the table. "Are you serious? You just want to march up and knock on his door?"

"Er ... yes?"

"Well, I'm going with you then."

"Fine. Good, I mean." I try a smile. "It'll be fine, I promise."

"Great. One more thing." Kat shuts the book in front of her, finally giving in to the conversation. "What if Emily *wasn't* buying drugs off him?"

"She looked pretty off this morning..." I say, thinking back to Emily's dirty hair, her sobs. "Definitely not her usual perfect self."

"OK, fair point," Kat agrees, "but what if..."

"Guys, I love you but I'm going to need you all to pipe the eff down." Taylor is taking notes so furiously I almost expect to see steam coming from her pen. "This is just not sinking in."

"Here, let me help..." Marcus attempts to look at the page and I jump a foot in the air as Taylor snatches the book from him and thumps the heavy cover shut, drawing glances from all sides. My stomach twinges at the sudden movement.

"I'm sorry," she stutters, "I didn't mean to. . ." Marcus's face is stony and she sighs, gathering up her things. "I'll be in my room."

I watch her leave the library, mouth slightly agape. Taylor never loses her composure, ever, no matter what. I wonder what's going on with her.

"I guess I'd better check on her," Marcus mumbles, shoving his own notes into his bag, throwing the strap over one shoulder, and standing up. "She's really feeling this workload. See you later, guys." He strides out of the door, taking a right as he follows Taylor's path.

"Is that a normal thing for them?" Cole asks as he stares at the doorway.

"No," I admit, leaning back in my chair to rub my stomach. "I've never seen her lose it at Marcus before," I say, bewildered. Another twinge of pain shoots through my stomach.

"Me either," agrees Kat. "But it is the final year. I don't know about you, but stuff is getting more complicated."

I eye the pile of textbooks about French political history I am yet to open and then look at Cole. *Complicated* seems like the right word.

"At least Emily hasn't shown up, right?" Kat says. "Although it would be interesting to talk to her. She was best friends with two of the victims."

"Yeah it would – ouch!" I break off and clutch my stomach.

Kat points at my midsection. "Make sure you get some painkillers on the way back up, won't you?"

"I have some upstairs." I take a deep breath to ease the pain. "I wonder what Emily is doing if she's not here, though." I shake my head. "She was so intense about wanting to show me something this morning."

"I was in the loo at lunch and heard one of the languages kids say she'd been sick in French," Kat says, her head back down in a collection of sonnets. "Maybe there's something going around."

"And you've only thought to tell me this now? I've spent the whole day dodging her!"

"Yeah, sorry. Slipped my mind. I thought she'd drag herself here no matter what after what you said, though. I hope she hasn't given you anything."

"Yeah, me too."

We sit in silence for a few minutes and I pretend to read, but it's no good. "I can't focus," I say, closing the book. "We need a plan." Cole and Kat follow suit and the three of us sit there for a second, thinking. "What are you both doing tomorrow afternoon?"

"Hockey," Kat says, at the same time as Cole shrugs. Wednesday afternoons are usually time for clubs and extra-curricular. I turn to Cole.

"If you're not signed up for anything yet, why don't we both go and see Creepy Billy tomorrow?"

"And say what?" Cole looks far from convinced, as if he regrets saying he'd come with me.

"I dunno, we can tell him we're doing an essay or something. I can show him my urban studies notes. It's only partly a lie."

"Listen, I know I said I'd go with you but I'm not so sure it's a good idea. I mean, Kat just saw him trading something with Emily, right? How do we know he's not involved in all this? I mean, why has he kept all that stuff? And if it's not cult related, he could still be dealing bad stuff to vulnerable people. Plus, his name has the word 'creepy' in it. I'm hardly eager to go knocking on his door."

"Although," Kat says, eyes still on her Shakespeare, "he could have been giving her *anything*."

"Like . . . information?" I say.

Kat nods. "I bet Creepy Billy sees and hears everything, you know."

Cole shakes his head and lets out a low groan. "Is this what it's always like, being surrounded by smart people? You don't get a second to breathe?"

"Pretty much." Kat shrugs, going back to her books.

"So, Cole," I say, tilting my head at him in what I hope is an irresistible way, "are you in?"

"Fine," he says, kissing me while Kat makes a yakking sound, "but only because it's for you."

28

The main corridors are quiet on a Wednesday afternoon. I nod and smile at the odd person wandering past in full-on Morton sports regalia, but the building seems deserted apart from that. Most people are off doing enrichment activities. It's compulsory in first year, but we can use the time to study as seniors if we want to, which is a blessing for someone who despises sports as much as I do. I relish the peace, having crawled through this morning's lessons after another night of tossing and turning.

My feet tap on the polished tiles of the entryway as I pace up and down, my black patent brogues making a swishing sound every time I stop and turn on the ball of my foot. I pause, arch my neck, and look up, the stairs empty for once rather than full of chattering teenagers. As ever, I'm taken aback by the grandeur of the entrance hall, the beautiful sweeping staircases that billow out and meet back again on the first floor below the huge, stained-glass window. At Christmas they put a six-metre-tall tree in the middle and decorate it with baubles bigger than my head. It's like something out of a fairy tale.

"OK there, daydreamer?" I blink at Cole's voice behind me and spin around.

"Hey! I was worried you'd forgotten about me." I catch his hand and point at the currently empty space. "Just looking forward to when they put the Christmas tree up, that's all. Wait 'til you see it, it's amazing."

"Cool." He loosens his tie slightly with his free hand. "How're you feeling?" I furrow my brow and tip my head as he rushes to explain. "You know, your, er, cramps. Feeling better?"

He's so thoughtful. "Yeah, all fine." I beam at him as he runs a finger around the inside of his shirt collar. The cramps eased last night, thankfully.

"God, it's boiling today – do we still have to wear uniform this afternoon?"

"Technically yes," I say, dropping his hand, "but I think you'll get away with being a bit more casual." I look him in the eye and slowly, deliberately, untuck my shirt. "See?"

"Oh, you maverick!" Cole cries as he makes a big deal

of shrugging off his blazer. "I don't know if I can handle the heady rebellion of it all!" I squeal and he lunges for me, nipping my waist with both hands. "See? The mere glimpse of an untucked shirt has sent me wild!"

"Stop," I try, between peals of laughter that leave me doubled over and breathless. I squirm away and catch my breath, dissolving into giggles again. "I hate being tickled."

"Really?" He grins wickedly, picking up his blazer from the floor. "I couldn't tell."

"Liar." I smile back as he offers me his hand again and I fold my fingers through his. They're cool and strong and send a glorious little chill up my arm.

"Are you sure you want to do this?"

"I am." I nod. I hold up the reporter's notepad and pen and give him my best perky smile. "Hi there, Mr Loomis, I was hoping to ask you some questions for a school project, would you mind?"

"Well, I'd answer your questions" – he drops a soft kiss on my cheek – "but I'm biased."

"Come on. The quicker we do this the better. I thought we could finish the tour of the back staircase once we were done."

Cole snaps to attention immediately. "Well, why didn't you say so?" He sweeps his free hand before us, gesturing to the double doors. "After you."

*

Even though I've seen Creepy Billy's – *Mr Loomis's*, I remind myself – house before, I always imagine it as run-down and derelict. However, the closer we get to it, I can see that it is immaculately kept. Hanging baskets decorate the red-brick walls, so that late summer flowers trail down either side of a painted black door that bears the hand-carved sign *Groundskeeper's Lodge* and there are window boxes full of tall, fragrant purple flowers with bleeding yellow hearts.

"Irises," Cole comments. The surprise must be evident on my face. "They're my mum's favourites. You don't usually see them in the autumn."

Oh, my heart.

"Hopefully he's home." I square my shoulders and paste a smile on, my hand poised to knock.

The door opens before my knuckles touch the wood.

"Wondered when one of you would show up," Creepy Billy grunts in the gloom of the cottage, "and now there's two of you. Well, come on in then, I suppose." He pauses to point at the irises. "Rebloomers. Come back before you go home for the holidays and I'll give you a cutting for your mother."

I turn to Cole as Mr Loomis shuffles away. His mouth is hanging open.

"Didn't expect that," he says.

"No, me neither." I glance at the open door.

"Come on then," Billy shouts from inside, "I haven't got all day."

I take a deep breath and step over the threshold, Cole on my heels. The cottage is small but clean and the stone floor is well swept. A small log fire smoulders in the corner of the little living room, making it stuffy and smoky but undeniably cosy.

Billy appears from behind another door with a pot of tea and three chipped tin mugs. "Sit down, then," he grumbles, setting them on the small wooden table before disappearing back into what I can only assume is the kitchen. Cole and I sit on the low, brown tweed sofa, a relic from the nineteen eighties by the looks of it.

Billy returns with a small carton of milk and some cubes of sugar. "Help yourselves, will you?" He sits slowly in the low-slung, worn armchair, the way older people whose joints are stiff and painful do, and grabs a poker from beside the fire.

"What do you need?" He doesn't look at us; instead he focuses on moving the coals around slowly, methodically.

"Erm, thanks for having us, Mr Loomis," I start, nodding at Cole to start pouring tea. "I was hoping to ask you some questions if that's OK? For a—"

"'Bout that ruddy cult, is it?" he interrupts and Cole's hand falters, spilling hot tea on to the wood. "Here." He pulls a rag from the pocket of his overalls and throws it at Cole. "Mop that up."

"How did you know that's what we'd ask about?" I ask,

my curiosity getting the better of me. No point in keeping up a charade if I don't have to.

"You finished?" Billy asks Cole, who nods and hands me a cup of steaming black tea. Billy leans forwards, close enough that I can see the grizzled grey of his stubble and the stains on his teeth. He grabs the teapot and fills his mug, grime-encrusted nails closing around two sugar cubes that he drops in with a splash. He follows with an unholy amount of milk, doesn't bother to stir, and leans back.

This time he fixes his eyes on me. "Was about time someone started digging about, if you ask me. Clever bunch of kids are bound to be curious and that nosy mare in the library let slip that she'd given someone that booklet with the clipping in. So." He stops to take a sip from his mug. "What exactly do you want to know?"

"I'm not really sure," I answer honestly. "We . . ." Cole shoots me a look. "Well, *I*, was hoping we might get a look at your, er, collection?"

"You mean the newspaper cuttings?"

"Yes! Do you really have them?"

Billy nods, scratching his chin, his nails scraping on the bristles there. "I do. They're not in any kind of order, though; you'll have to do that yourself."

"That's fine!" I fail to keep the excitement out of my voice. "Can I ask – why did you keep them?"

"Hate seeing history thrown away," he explains,

slurping from his mug. "Been here longer than any of you lot. People want to come in and change the history of this place to suit themselves and it just don't work like that. You got to know your history if you don't want to repeat it, 'specially the bad stuff. This headmistress isn't the first one to do it, so I keep whatever they chuck and return it all when a new head takes over." He drains his cup as his words sink in. Creepy Billy, unofficial archivist of Morton Academy. "You ready then? Leave them cups here, don't want you spilling on anything."

"Of course." I set down my untouched mug and stand, Cole following suit, though I can see he's politely drunk his tea, too.

Billy pushes himself up into a standing position. "I'm working on the allotment this afternoon, just out there." He points a gnarled finger back towards the front door. "So you can stay for a bit. Just stay out of the other room, that's mine, so it is. No need to be going in there anyway."

"Of course," Cole says. "We'll respect your privacy." Billy appraises him and nods.

"Good. You got an hour, then I'm back in for another brew and a sit-down, so I expect you to be done by then."

"Of course, thanks C . . . Mr Loomis."

"Call me Billy." He smiles, though it's full of browning teeth rather than humour. "Just drop the Creepy, will you? I'm a flamin' pussycat."

"Uh, thank you, Billy." Cole and I exchange wide-eyed

looks as we follow him through a narrow hallway and into the kitchen. Like the small front room, it is bright and clean, well-scrubbed but simple. There are three doors in here – the one on the back wall is propped open and leads to a small, pretty garden, which must be Billy's private space. The others are to the left, side by side on the whitewashed stone wall. We follow Billy to one and he pulls it open before walking off without another word.

"Holy..." Cole breathes, before dissolving into a loud cough.

I couldn't have said it better myself.

The tiny box room is in stark contrast to the rest of the house. The small space is cramped and dusty, brown file boxes piled haphazardly on top of one another, most of them towering over me. By the looks of things, there was an awful lot of stuff Patel wanted rid of when she was put in charge.

"Ready to dive in?" I ask.

"Let's do it," Cole responds, before immediately sneezing three times in a row.

29

"You know, you'd think all that sniffling would get annoying, but you still look very cute."

Cole glares at me over his open box of newspaper clippings. The air is hot, humid, and thick with dust motes; his eyes are red-rimmed and streaming. "I'm fine," he says defensively, sniffing loudly. "We'll be done soon, right?"

"I hope so." I thump the lid down on my own box and heft it out of the way, causing another wave of dust to fill the little room. "Oops, sorry!" I squeak as Cole lets off another volley of sneezes.

"I hope so too." He uses the sleeve of his shirt to wipe

his forehead and a trail of grey dirt comes away on the previously white sleeve.

"Here, one second, let me grab you a tissue."

"No," he sniffles, "I'm fine, honestly—" He's cut off by a barrage of sneezes and sighs. "OK. Thank you."

"One minute," I promise him. I stand and wipe my own dust-laden, sweaty palms on my checked skirt, the dirt blending in with the tweedy fabric. I'm sure I saw a door in the little hallway between the front room and kitchen – that has to be the bathroom.

I sneak back through the kitchen, half afraid Billy will come back and think I'm snooping. I'm right, though, there's a small bathroom off the corridor, barely large enough to swing a cat in, though thankfully as clean as the rest of the cottage.

I wash my hands in cool, soapy water, my eyes drifting around the room. It's pretty stark apart from a small ledge of plants on the windowsill above the sink, all in terracotta pots with little lollipop sticks stuck into the soil. I grab a piece of tissue to blot my hands and lean a little closer to see if I can make out the writing, but it's all smudged where the wood has swollen over timeless waterings and the letters are not familiar enough to recognize.

"Belladonna, Camphor and Castor." Billy's gruff voice invades my thoughts and I jump, realizing the door is still wide open.

"You scared me!" I put a still damp hand to my heart,

which is racing. "I'm sorry, I was just washing my hands," I say, words spilling out over each other. "It's dusty in there."

"Humph," he says, "long as you're not snooping." He nods to the plants. "Hard to grow those and they're poisonous. Don't touch 'em."

"I won't." I look back at the plants for a second. "Why do you grow them, if they're poisonous?"

"I like a challenge," he says. "Now, if you don't mind..." I stand awkwardly before I realize he probably wants to use his own bathroom.

"Oh! Sorry." I grab some more tissue and hold it up. "For Cole. He has allergies. All the dust, you know."

"Humph," Billy says again as I hurry past him. "You got twenty minutes," he calls after me.

"What was all that?" Cole asks as I re-enter the room and gently close the door. His eyes are practically shut now and I feel awful that he's sat through all this to help me, especially when he could have been off signing up for football.

"Here, that's enough." I clear a space by the window, open it wide and guide him to it. "I just saw Billy, he said we've got twenty minutes, so I'll just speed-read anything that's left while you sit here. He's growing some crazy plants in his bathroom..." Cole raises an eyebrow and I laugh. "No, not that kind. Though I wouldn't mind a closer look at his allotment one night..."

"Don't you dare. Crazy like how?"

200

"Poisonous stuff, like belladonna. A couple of others too, castor and camphor, maybe?" I search in my bag and produce an almost empty bottle of water, pouring a little on to some of the tissues. "Here. Lean against the wall and put these on your eyes." He doesn't argue, just does as I say. A low moan escapes his lips.

"Ohhh, that's better." He murmurs.

"Good." I leave him sitting by the window and start on the boxes we have yet to root through. I'm about a third of the way down one of the last boxes when I see something interesting. "Hey, I think I've got something."

"You do?" Cole lifts the pads of tissue from his eyes and uses them to wipe the little bits of black dust gunk that have gathered in the corners. "Yuk. I need to wash my face."

"Five more minutes." I set the book aside and go through the rest of the box. Nothing. A quick check of the remaining two storage boxes doesn't turn up anything else. "I think that's it."

"Really? Thank God." He starts to climb to his feet, the tissue screwed up and useless in his hand.

"Wait a sec, let me see if I'm right." I pick up the thick, leather-bound volume that I set aside. It's one of those old photo albums, the pages inside sticky and covered in plastic. But instead of pictures, the book is crammed with newspaper clippings – specifically *The Prescott Times, 1999–2000*.

"Here." Cole collects his blazer and bag from the floor

and opens the flap that covers the top of his satchel. "Let's borrow it." He takes it from me without another word and slides it into his bag, throwing his blazer across the top.

"Cole!" Is he serious? "We can't, it's stealing!"

"No, it's not," he argues, "it's borrowing. We'll give it back when we're done; it's not like he'll notice."

"I don't know..."

"Well, I do. Come on, goody-two-shoes." He leaves the room and I have no real choice but to follow him. We leave the cottage and pass Billy grafting on the allotment at the front, tending to the berries that I realize he must use to make his famous jam. The long, sharp garden fork in his hand gleams in the sunlight.

"Thank you." I wave. He nods and grunts and that's it. Poor Billy. He's less creepy and more lonely, I think.

"I can't believe we just did that," I gasp as we enter the cool space of the entrance hall. It's still early and sports don't finish for another hour at least.

"Sorry, I couldn't survive much longer in that room," Cole apologizes, looking down at his shirt. "Jeez, I'm filthy." He draws a finger across my forehead and pulls it away, coated in dust. "And so are you."

"Ewww! Right, let's go and get cleaned up. Why don't we go for a shower..."

"We?" He grins and I poke him in the chest.

"Separate showers, obviously, and then meet in the girls' lounge upstairs? No one goes in there any more..."

"OK," he says more sombrely. "Give me twenty minutes." We climb the stairs together and pause under the huge window, its rainbow lights dancing on the stone steps. "See you soon."

"See you soon." He waves before walking away to the stairs that lead up to the boys' dorms. I head the other way, dreaming of a hot shower. I hear him sneezing all the way down the hallway.

I don't realize how filthy I am until I watch the scummy grey foam slope down my feet and into the shower drain. Yuk.

I close my eyes and enjoy the solitude for a second, tilting my head forwards so the water trickles down my back. I have the whole bathroom to myself, so the water is actually hot and there are no unidentified hairs here before me, which is both nice and unusual. Sharing a bathroom with so many girls wasn't ideal, but I was used to it – I'd never had much privacy at home either. I think of the private bathroom upstairs in the head girl's room. Lucky Taylor!

I crank the handle into the off position and shiver as the cold air hits immediately, grabbing the huge, fluffy white towel from the hook on the door. I shroud myself in it and emerge in a cloud of steam, feet sliding around in my flip-flops as I carry my little shower bag over to the bank of mirrors.

I catch sight of myself through the mist and do a double-take. I lean in, wiping away the steam, letting my fingers trail along the mirror and push wet strands of hair away from my face. I look . . . healthy. Healthier than I've looked in ages. My eyes are bright and my cheeks are flushed and I watch a huge smile spread across my face as I think of why or, more accurately, *who* is responsible for the change.

I reflect on the last few days. Despite the truly awful things that have happened, despite the fear and worry and heartbreak . . . I am actually *happy*. I'm back at Morton, something I worried all summer might not happen.

And then there's Cole. I watch as my smile gets even brighter.

I pull my comb out of the shower bag and brush my hair back before parting it down the centre, fat drops of water rolling down my shoulders. I grab another towel from the fresh pile on the counter and tip my head forwards, starting to rough dry my hair. As I do so, I hear the main bathroom door open and shut.

"Hi," I call, to let whoever it is know that someone's in here. "I'm almost done." I blot my hair some more, until it stops dripping on me, pack up my things, including a little pot of Kat's Tiger Balm that's somehow made its way into my stuff, and head to the door.

The air is still steamy – I may have gone a little overboard with the temperature in the shower earlier – and I can't see anyone else in here. Did I imagine the sound of the door just then? Or did it close in the wind or something?

"Hello?" I try again, feeling ridiculous. Nothing.

I start towards the door again and realize I've left my shower bag behind. Christ – I forget the simplest things these days. If it's not written down, whether it's homework or taking my meds, it doesn't happen. I turn back to the mirrors, clutching my towel around me, the steam clearing slightly. My bag comes into focus, right where I left it. And then, so does the mirror.

Alongside the clear patch I wiped in the glass, there are words, enormous, dripping words that run from the top to the bottom of the mirror. I squint, reading them, then I grab my bag, spin on my heel and run. But not before the message is seared into my brain, one I know I won't forget.

"Hey." Cole is already waiting for me as I run up the spiral staircase to the seniors' lounge. "Hey," he repeats, his voice laced with concern, "what's up? Did something happen?"

I don't answer. Instead I run over and throw my arms around him, pressing my face into his chest. He pulls me away. "Whoa, you're soaking! Liz, tell me what happened."

I blurt out the whole story. By the time I'm done, I'm out of breath. "It was just ... freaky. Like it appeared out of nowhere. I thought I was on my own but. . ." I trail off. "You don't believe me, do you?"

"Believe what?" Kat's cheerful voice echoes across from the staircase. "What have you been up to, Lizzie?" She grins, wagging a finger. Then she gets a good look at my face. "What's happened?"

I fill her in, starting to shiver as I do so. I'd raced back to my room and pulled on the nearest things I could find, and I now realize my thin T-shirt is soaking wet.

"I'll go and have a look," she says, heading back down the stairs. "Liz, change into this." She chucks an oversized hoody in my direction and disappears. I shiver again.

"Go on then, do what you need to do." Cole makes a big show of covering his eyes. "I won't peek, promise."

"Er, I'll just go into Taylor's room." I am suddenly very aware that my T-shirt is now incredibly see-through and hold the hoody across myself as I dart to the room. Thankfully, it's open. "Hello?" I try, just in case, but the room is empty, as it has been all week.

I shrug out of the wet tee. Taylor's hairdryer has made it up here, so I give my now-damp bra a good blast on the hot setting before sliding Kat's jumper on over my head. The thick fleece inside feels like velvet on my bare skin, so different from my thin cheapo one. Not that there's anything wrong with mine, I remind myself – I can just tell this one is more expensive. It comes down past my thighs and I push the sleeves up to my elbows, noticing that the coral colour brightens up my face. I start to blow-dry my hair, my bones warming though as I do so, before flipping it back and brushing it through with Taylor's paddle brush.

"Hey, that's better!" Cole smiles as I emerge, opening his arms for another hug. "Mmm, much better," he mumbles into my warm hair. I close my eyes and allow myself to settle for a moment but it doesn't last long. I can hear the sound of feet on metal steps ringing around the room.

"Hey." Kat emerges and I can tell by the look on her face that I'm not going to want to hear what she has to say. "Feeling better?"

I ignore the question. "Did you see it?" I break away from Cole and start to fiddle with my sleeves, dragging them down past my knuckles. My thumbs find little holes made to poke through, so I do, relishing the feeling of safety it provides.

"Come on," Kat says kindly, her eyes darting over my head to look at Cole. "Let's sit down."

"What? No." I look between the two of them. "I'm not a child. Just tell me."

"Well, there was nothing there." Kat's face is apologetic but I can't help it – I start to laugh. It's hollow, though, strange and flat.

"It was written in steam, Kat! Someone could have wiped it away, or the cleaners came in, or – or it just – I don't know, evaporated or something. You know . . ." I make a poofing gesture with both hands. "Science!"

She's quiet, head down, not quite avoiding my eyes but not meeting them either. I turn to Cole. "You believe me, don't you?"

"Of course I do." He says it with such conviction I feel buoyed for a second.

"Thank you," I whisper.

"Lizzie, I believe you, too," Kat says, her voice quiet. "I'm just . . . scared. I don't know if this thing is over. . ."

"Or if it's only just beginning? I know," I whisper. I hold my hand out to her. She comes over and takes it. "I'm sorry. Come on, you're right, we need to sit down."

We choose the leather sofas closest to Taylor's room and sink into them. It's only then I realize Cole has his schoolbag with him.

"I almost forgot," I say. "Do you have it?"

"Have what?" Kat asks, stretching her legs out, taking up an entire two-seater as she flips her trainers off and props her feet on the arm. She's got a different hoody on now, this one creamy against her olive skin. "Shall I text the others, tell them what happened? Where we are?"

"Yeah, good idea." Cole tugs the book from his satchel and I notice that his initials are carved into the leather of the bag. "A leaving gift," he explains, following my gaze, "from my mum. To say congrats. You know what mums are like."

"That's so cute," I say, trying to think of the last thing my mum gave me, apart from a hard time.

"They're on their way." Kat's little silver flip phone disappears into a pocket and she sits up. "Come on then, let's forget about threatening messages and talk about murder cults." Her voice only holds a trace of sarcasm. "What have you two been up to?"

I explain as Cole pulls a packet of antibacterial wipes from his bag and starts wiping the dust from the cover. "Poor Cole was allergic to everything." I smile at him, his eyes still faintly red. "But he soldiered on and then, uh, borrowed this book. Billy didn't give us much time, so I haven't looked properly, but the dates are right."

"Dates are right for what?" Taylor and Marcus appear at the top of the stairs, both dressed in baggy pants and hoodies, though Taylor's is cropped so it shows off her tanned stomach. They look ridiculously cute and matchy. I realize this means Marcus has not even bothered sneaking over the wall this time – he's come up the stairs through the girls' dorms. It looks like they've stopping caring if they're caught or not.

"For the murder cult," I explain, beckoning them over. Cole pushes the now clean book into the centre of the low coffee table and I slide off my seat, scooting on to the floor and settling myself between his legs. I pat the space next to me and Taylor shuffles close, Marcus taking the seat behind her. A curtain of red hair hangs over her cheek. "Hey," I say quietly, "how's the scratch?"

"Rank," she sighs, pushing the hair behind her ear. The scratch is more of a wound now, the edges crusting beneath the heavy foundation she's tried to hide it with. It looks painful.

"Oh, honey," I sympathize, "have you been to see the nurse? I bet she could give you something for it."

"No, I've been too busy, but I will. So." She changes the subject swiftly as Kat and I exchange worried glances. "Fill us in."

At this rate, Taylor is going to burn out. Still, maybe being head girl requires this sort of dedication. I tip my head backwards to look at Cole. "Your turn."

Cole repeats the events of the afternoon. I'm itching to start looking through the cuttings. "There might not be anything in there," Cole finishes, "but it was the only thing that looked promising, so..."

"So let's look at it, my God, I am dying of suspense!" Kat blurts out and flips the cover, which breaks the tension I had not quite realized was there.

"OK." I laugh. "Let's look."

Kat scoots around the table to my left side and we start to flip through, the five of us scouring each page. They're all local newspaper cuttings about Morton – mostly what you'd expect. Outstanding exam results, local community work, Oxbridge acceptances, that sort of thing. Some alumni stuff too, soirees where Morton old boys and girls came back to showcase their success and donate towards the future of the school. Every one of them would have been through Jewel and Bone, I think. It is one of these pieces, dated September 1999 and accompanied with a smudged black-and-white photograph, that makes Kat grab my hand so I don't turn the page.

"Look at the caption," she whispers.

"'*Nikhita Patel*,'" Marcus reads aloud, "'*Head Girl of Morton Academy, greets Old Boy Bradley Harrison, CEO of Transcendental Health Enterprises*.'"

31

"Wait," Marcus says excitedly, leaning over Taylor again, both hands on her shoulders. "That was the name of that guy, the cult guy!"

We all peer round at him. "Babe," Taylor sighs, patting him on the knee, "for someone so smart, you can be a total himbo."

"Sexist," Marcus grumbles, leaning back. "It's him, though, right?"

"Definitely," I agree, "and *that*" – I point to the smiling girl shaking his hand – "is Dr Patel."

"I don't believe it," Kat breathes, looking up at the roll call of past head girls on the wall. Jameela's photograph is up there now, too. I hadn't realized. Her smile is wide, proud. She looks as though she has the world at her feet.

My stomach flips. That's it. *That's* Jameela's legacy: a photo on a wall in a school that hardly anyone will see.

"There she is." I point Dr Patel out to Cole. Her hair is long, dark and parted to one side, her cheeks flushed and fresh, brown eyes smiling. There's a small golden plaque beneath the frame engraved with her name and the date "1999–2000". She looks pretty much the same apart from the fact the girl in the picture looks happy.

"Dr Patel never smiles these days," I murmur.

"Maybe it's Botox," Taylor says. "Plus I reckon she's had some fillers – her lips looked suspiciously thinner when she was eighteen, don't you think?"

"She can't be more than forty," Cole says, looking at the date of the photo. "Pretty young to be a principal, then?"

"I suppose so."

"Come on, is there any more?" Taylor nudges me impatiently. I flip through the pages carefully, scanning the clippings. They are brittle, starting to crackle with age. You can tell they haven't been looked after properly for a few years.

"Bor-ing," Marcus groans.

"Wait!" I stop towards the end of the book, another pixelated photo of Bradley Harrison gazing out from the page. He's wearing a tuxedo and holding a brandy glass in one hand. The background makes it clear that this picture was also taken here, at Morton. He was clearly a donor. I wonder if he was a Jewel and Bone sponsor, too? Even though he's in a sea of people, some kind of event happening around him, his eyes have managed to find the camera. Stubble covers his cheeks and lower jaw. You can see that he must have been good looking at some point, but this picture looks more like a mugshot, his eyes dark and penetrating and his mouth twisted into a privileged white-boy smirk.

"God, I hate his face," Kat murmurs.

"'*Bradley Harrison*,'" I read aloud, "'*CEO of Transcendental Health Enterprises, is being sought for questioning by local police after a spate of suspicious deaths last month*.'" I check the date on the top of the clipping – the thirteenth of October 1999. "'*The former Morton Academy head boy has been linked to the alleged murders, amongst rumours of cult-related activities. This is the most recent photograph of the suspect, taken at an event at Morton Academy last month. Police advise that you should not approach him directly but instead call the hotline number below.*'"

"Jeez," Kat whispers. "That's horrible." Her eyes are glittering. "Keep going."

I flip the page but Bradley Harrison's face is etched into my eyelids and I see his sneer every time I blink. "Look." I point at two small, formal-looking clippings on the next page. "Obituaries."

They're worded similarly, both lamenting the passing of someone young. People who have left Morton and gone on to great things, only for their lives to be "snuffed out". A couple more of these phrases jump out, most notably "unexpected and sudden death" and "ongoing investigation".

"Come on, then, resident true-crime guru," I say to Kat. "Are we talking murder?"

"Oh, def murdered," she says, brushing her unruly hair behind one ear and leaning closer. Her hair is drying and starting to curl and wave, the exact opposite to my limp spaghetti strings from earlier. "If there's an investigation into the death, that's never a good thing."

I flip to the next page. We're nearing the end of the book now and I'm starting to worry this is all we'll find out.

But I'm wrong.

"Bingo," I breathe.

Every single body around me leans in as we absorb the double-page spread. This one is dated June 2000 and clearly taken from a red-top tabloid rather than the local paper. *MURDER CULT LEADER FOUND GUILTY* screams the headline, and another photo of Bradley Harrison is splashed across the page. This time he looks gaunt and unkempt, flanked by police officers, hands cuffed firmly behind his back.

"Just – wait a second." Taylor puts a hand on the page, as though she wants to unsee the article. "What are we doing? Things have been tragic enough around here recently, let's just take this to. . ." She stops.

"To who?" I press. "Dr Patel? The police?"

"I don't like this," whimpers Taylor. We ignore her; this is too important.

"In true crime there are no coincidences," Kat says. "Look." She points at the article and begins to read aloud. "*'Though Harrison was not found guilty of murder himself, he was charged with coercion and conspiracy to murder. The surviving members of the cult have stated that Harrison was the driving force behind the slayings, telling followers that if they sacrificed another human being, they would reap the benefits in power and wealth.'*"

"That is twisted," Cole murmurs. "What about *him*, though? What was *he* going to get out of all this?"

"His rivals out of the way, maybe?" Kat replies. "These psychos are always way too clever. They pull the strings and watch the fallout. Revel in it, even. I told you, it's like Charles Manson. He made people do all sorts of terrible stuff, but never got his own hands dirty." She taps the newsprint. "Sounds like our boy Bradley did the same thing, and listen to this." She points to a line and reads aloud. "*'Harrison was sentenced to life imprisonment. However, he will potentially be eligible for parole in 2019.'*"

"You're kidding," I breathe. "That means he could be out now? Like, around here?"

"Yep." Kat stands and stretches, making her way back to the empty sofa. "And even worse," she says as she sits, "look at the way those poor people died."

I glance back at the article and see a small box in the corner. It lists names, ages, and manners of death – for easy reading, I think in disgust. Tabloids are gross.

"Drowning, poison, bludgeoning and ... stabbing," I read out. "*Harrison's followers believed that the more traumatic the death, the greater their reward would be.*'"

"That is so messed up," Taylor mutters, easing herself up from the floor to sit on Marcus's lap, curling up in a ball as though he can protect her from the idea. "Why would people believe him?"

"Cult leaders prey on the vulnerable," Kat explains. "Harrison would have told them everything they wanted to hear. Things they'd ached to hear their whole lives. Told them they were special, important, beloved..."

"I kind of get it," Cole says quietly. "I mean, who doesn't want to be told they're worth something? That something they do will be remembered, their sacrifices worthwhile?"

Silence descends upon us like a thick layer of snow. We *all* get it, to a point. After all, that's why we're here, at Morton.

"Anyway," Kat breaks the silence, "we can't deny there's an awful lot of similarity between these crimes and the events of the last few days. And weeks, if we count Morgan."

"Let's not get carried away just yet," Marcus says. "I still need to check what that was in Jameela's inhaler before we can say for certain. I can't do it until we get internet access this weekend – I've not been able to find the right books anywhere."

No one says anything. We all know it was poison.

"He could be out now," I say, and my voice sounds very small. "He could be anywhere, even here. They could be working together."

"Bradley Harrison on the loose," Kat sighs, "yet another thing we need the internet for. Stupid burner phones. God, I miss the twenty-first century sometimes."

"Guys," Cole says. "You've missed out the last line. Listen: *'The prosecution hinged on the words of one surviving member of the cult, another former student of Morton Academy. Rikesh Patel explained how Harrison had brainwashed him into attempting to kill his own sister, so that he could achieve the success that had evaded him since he left the school.'*"

"His *sister*?" Kat sits up, her gaze travelling to the wall of headshots.

"Yep." Cole nods. "His sister, head girl at Morton Academy. Nikhita Patel."

32

"Well," Kat says, letting out a breath. "You guys certainly brought us some serious information."

"Hmm." I'm not fully listening. I trail my fingers over the final page in the book. It's empty but the plastic overlay is crinkled and there are traces of newsprint on the sticky surface beneath.

"You think there was something here?" Cole says, his gaze alert.

"Maybe." I frown, trying to think. "Emily said she had something to show us. . ."

"And do you think it's whatever was here?"

"What if we've been thinking about this all wrong?"

I say. I flip back a couple of pages and tap the photo of Patel with Harrison. "This proves they at least met, and he doesn't seem to be much older than her, really. What if Dr Patel was involved in the cult, rather than just being a victim of it? What if . . ." I take a deep breath and close my eyes. "What if the cult *was* the school? What if it was Jewel and Bone, just under another name?"

I open my eyes and their expressions are wide and shocked but not disbelieving.

"No," Taylor murmurs.

"Dr Patel got rid of this stuff," I say. "We know she was head girl at the time of the Transcendent Faithful and that she was at least aware of Harrison before that. We know he was a head boy and he came back to Morton for events – like sponsorship dinners – so he must have been part of Jewel and Bone, right? All Morton successes belonged to it – still do."

"Yeah, they do," Kat says around a mouthful of bitten nails. "I mean, that's why we're all in it, right?"

Five heads nod around the table.

"It's why I am," I say, thinking about my parents' tiny flat. "I need to get out of the cesspit I grew up in." Cole squeezes my shoulder and I lean back, feeling safe for a second.

"Me too," Marcus agrees. "I want to be a doctor, help people. There was no chance that was happening for me at home."

"Babe, don't worry about the past." Taylor kisses him on the cheek. "You'll be the world's hottest doctor. I wanted out, too. We all did."

"How exactly does this society set you on the path to success? Or is this something I should have asked before starting the hunt?" Cole asks. I keep forgetting he's the new boy.

"The school was founded—" I'm interrupted by the corner of a cushion landing in my open mouth along with a series of groans.

"History lesson alert," Kat yells, dodging the pillow as I stand up and toss it back to her.

"As I was saying," I carry on, moving around to the other sofa and sitting down opposite Cole, "Patrick Morton founded the academy in 1906. It was a pretty common thing to do back then; philanthropy was a big deal to the rich folk who had nothing better to spend their fortunes on. Anyway, he realized he could do more than educate the clever kids he was bankrolling – he could ensure lifelong success if he put them in touch with the right people – successful people. So he decided to set up an offshoot of the secret society he was a part of."

"The Society of Odd Fellows," Kat chimes in. "Winston Churchill was one, you know."

"Very good, Katerina!" I pat her knee as she wrinkles her nose at the use of her full name. "Yeah, so he started his own kind of junior offshoot. He'd found Old Josef . . .

somewhere. And since the Odd Fellows used to conduct their meetings around a human skeleton, he decided he would, too. Ours was supposedly an old saint and therefore covered in precious stones, so, eventually the members' nickname of Jewel and Bone stuck, rather than the pretty long-winded original: the Philanthropic Junior Chapter of the Society of Odd Fellows."

"Right." Cole sweeps the hair from his forehead and I spot a little frown line between his eyes. It's cute. "So we're actually part of this bigger society?"

"Yeah, which is why people go on to do so well. That original society has members everywhere. It's why we're practically guaranteed entry into any red-brick university we want and, as long as we put the work in, we will succeed." I tap the book. "Just like Bradley Harrison did."

"Before he lost it," Taylor mumbles.

"I am starting to wish I'd looked it up now, though." Cole laughs nervously. "Instead of just saying yes."

"You wouldn't have found anything, mate." Marcus presses a closed fist to Cole's arm. "I'm glad you're my deputy. We weren't betting on all" – he spreads his hands wide – "this."

"None of us were," Kat says. "Plus none of us really knew what we were getting ourselves into, either. We had notes pinned to our pillow last year, just like you did, then we had the official welcome ceremony followed by that stupid initiation and—"

"Initiation?" Cole interrupts. "No one told me anything about an initiation."

"That's because they were banned," I explain, "after last summer."

"Last summer..." Realization washes over his face. "That girl, the one in the lake..."

"Morgan," Taylor whispers, glancing up at the wall from where the dead girls watch us.

"She died doing an initiation?"

We all nod, avoiding one another's eyes.

"It was her own fault," whispers Kat, her voice stripped of its usual confidence. "She made us take the boats out, wearing blindfolds. I mean, look at us – we're hardly posh, none of us are sailors, are we? I doubt most of us even saw the sea when we were growing up, let alone learned how to manoeuvre a sailboat. Anyway, there was a collision, on the lake. It was windy and we were all hyped up, invincible, you know? There were like, eighteen of us, all acolytes, all giddy as anything. It was carnage." Kat sighs, reliving the night. "But then the sailboats crashed and the boom on one of the boats went wild – it swung across and hit Liz and Morgan on the head, throwing them into the water and tipping the boat up."

"Morgan went in first." I take up the story, my voice quivering at the memory. "I remember the splash. Before I could pull my blindfold off I was smashed in the head – I felt like one of those old cartoons, stars and tweety birds flying all around my head." I raise my hand to the scar along my scalp. "Split my head open. I wasn't unconscious, though – I managed to cling to the upturned boat until someone came for me. But Morgan must have been. She was gone, floating face down in the water, drifting further and further out to the middle of the lake." I choke out the last words and they taste of stagnant lake water. "That's all I remember."

"Wait, where was Patel during all this?" Cole says. "Did she know what you were doing?"

"She wasn't there, until ... after. When we dragged Morgan from the lake to the chapel, that's when Patel appeared," Taylor explains.

"How do you know that for sure?" Cole says, his expression intent. "You were all blindfolded, weren't you?"

Taylor shrugs. "I guess we don't. God, this all makes the motto sound really sick, now."

"Motto?" Cole asks.

"*Non fortuna nisi per sacrificium*," she says, burying her head into Marcus's shoulder. "*Behind success lies sacrifice.*" Those words ring so differently now.

I've read that somewhere – very recently.

"That's exactly what Bradley Harrison's followers believed," I realize, pulling the book around to this side of the table and skimming the article again. "Here." I start to read the reporter's words aloud. "'*Harrison seemingly wanted his disciples to believe that their murderous acts would gain them*

225

a higher place in society – that their sacrifices would create success for them later. Reports on Harrison urging members to name him on their life insurance policies are currently unfounded.'" I bet he made them hand over everything and then planned for someone to kill them, too."

"You know what we have to do now, don't you?" Kat says, eyes twinkling. Oh, God, I already know whatever she's thinking is a bad idea.

"Find out if Patel was part of the cult," Marcus says softly.

"Find out if Patel was part of the cult." Kat confirms.

"How are we going to do that?" I ask, turning to face Kat. I'm still wrapped in her hoody.

"We break into her office."

Everyone looks stunned, horrified, and then, slowly, we all nod.

"Fine," I agree. "But first you have to help me find out what Creepy Billy was giving to Emily."

33

"I cannot believe you have talked us into this," Taylor grumbles from her spot behind the low wall.

"Shush, he'll hear us," I hiss. "You can moan at me later."

"Oh, I will," she says, but thankfully falls silent.

All four of us are crouched behind the little stone wall that rings the allotment. It's dark and we are dressed all in black, per Kat's instructions. On the other side of the wall, Mr Loomis potters about his plants — although why he's doing it in the dark is anyone's guess.

A strong hand circles my waist and I slap it playfully but let it stay. "You make a very hot cat-burglar," Cole murmurs.

"Behave," I whisper, but I don't tell him to move. His arm pulls me a little closer.

"Spoilsport."

"Jesus, get a room," Kat says. Even though it was my idea, she has taken this *very* seriously, down to the black lines smeared across her cheeks. Camouflage, apparently. "We're already a man down. Where *is* Marcus, anyway?"

Taylor shrugs and pouts, looking down at her nails. "Ringing home, I think. I don't know."

"Get down!" I snap. We lie in a jumble of arms and legs, our bodies pressed tight to the wall as a beam of light sweeps over us.

"Mr Loomis?"

"Who's that?" Kat hisses from somewhere near my left knee. "I can't hear properly."

"Because you've got your face in my chest," Taylor says and Kat giggles.

"Sorry, wondered what that was."

I ease myself out of Cole's grip and poke my head over the wall, just a tiny bit. I'm grateful Kat made me wear a hat now – my blonde hair would be glowing otherwise.

"Mr Loomis," the voice repeats. "Whatever are you doing out here so late?"

"It's Dr Patel," I whisper and Kat swears.

"We're dead if she catches us."

Maybe literally.

"Some plants don't like the daylight too much," he

replies. From here I can see the flash of some lethal-looking shears, followed by the sound of water spilling from a metal can. "They like to be watered after dark. Funny things, plants."

"Quite," Dr Patel replies.

"What can I do for you, doctor?" Mr Loomis's voice seems to carry a touch of irritation now. I squint to get a good look at the plants but honestly, I have no idea what I'm looking at. They could be marijuana or chrysanthemums for all I know. In the corner of each eye I see the others untangle themselves and join me.

We all peer over the wall. If anyone looked our way, there would be four little pairs of eyes floating at the top of the wall. I suddenly remember playing Whac-A-Mole as a kid and stifle a giggle. How is it possible to be amused while my body is a twisting pit of anxiety? It must be nerves.

"Oh, nothing, I'm just out for a . . . stroll. It's a lovely evening."

"Right. Well." He points the shears towards the floor, moonlight glinting on the blades. "You should watch yourself in those shoes out here. Dangerous on an allotment in the dark."

"Thank you, Mr Loomis." Dr Patel's voice is ice cold. "Is that you finished for the evening?"

There's a pause. "S'pose so," he tuts, clearly dismissed from his own turf. He gathers up his watering can. "I'll drop your herbal tea off in the morning, as normal. New blend. Couple of the kiddos have had some off me this week; they've had trouble sleeping as well – what with all the . . . you know."

"Yes, thank you, Mr Loomis," Dr Patel repeats and we all watch him retreat to his cottage.

"Tea?" Taylor hisses. "Emily was getting *tea* off him?"

Minutes that feel like hours tick by. Sharp gravel cuts into my knees.

The headmistress doesn't move.

"What is Dr Patel playing at?" Cole whispers.

I shrug.

"Is she nicking plants or something? Poisonous ones?" Taylor asks, dropping back on the floor. Her back is pressed against the wall, facing towards the main school building. I keep watching the allotment and, beyond it, the gates that the delivery vans use.

That's when I see him. Walking through the gates, brazen as you like.

"Oh my GOD."

Dr Patel's head whips in our direction, but we're already in another human puddle on the ground.

"Did you see him? Did you?" I sound delirious, even to myself.

"Who?" Taylor asks, untangling herself again.

"Look."

The four of us move as one, each head bobbing up

230

within a millisecond of another. I almost expect Dr Patel to be standing there holding a mallet. But she's talking in a low voice to the figure I saw.

"Oh, hell no," Kat murmurs. "Is that. . .?"

"Yes," I breathe. "It's her brother. Rikesh Patel is alive, well and in the grounds of Morton Academy."

34

In theory, the plan seems reasonably straightforward. Except that we've no choice but to execute it on one of the busiest days in Morton's calendar. Plus, if we blow it, we've ruined our only chance.

No pressure.

It's the day of open evening, so we've had the afternoon off lessons to prepare, to make sure Morton looks its sparkling best for the prospective candidates. Most will arrive with their parents, wide-eyed fifteen- and sixteen-year-olds clutching their ivory-coloured invitations, all hand-selected by Dr Patel and the board of governors. They will probably never have seen a place like this before, apart from on television. Banners are up, uniforms have been pressed and a sheaf of letter-headed revision cards sit snugly in my top pocket, just in case I forget the name of the artist who created the stained-glass window, or what year the main staircase was added. I'm spending the first part of the evening on meet and greet duties and then I'll be leading tours at six and seven for the prospective history candidates.

I find the others in the common room, the only area that will be out of bounds to visitors tonight – we'll show them the junior one, but this is where we can come in between tours for a break. Even our bedrooms will be on show. Taylor finally agreed to relocate to the head girl's bedroom, it would look odd if it didn't look lived in, but she wasn't thrilled about the prospect of sleeping on her own.

"Are we ready for this?" I ask.

"I think so." Kat is scribbling down times and initials on a scrappy piece of paper, her cake untouched. She *must* be taking this seriously. I scooch in next to Cole and feel a little tug of happiness when I see that he's made me a mug of Earl Grey.

"Thank you," I murmur, pecking his cheek before taking a sip, the powerful citrus aroma sliding down the back of my throat, coating it in perfume.

"You're welcome." He smiles, sliding one hand on to my leg without thinking. We both freeze for a second, it's

233

still all so new, but when I melt into him I feel his muscles relax, too. I take another sip of tea and try to avoid the fact we're planning to break into the headteacher's office. "One more time." I address the group. "What's the plan?"

"It's half four now," Kat starts. I glance at my watch and nod. "The first tours arrive at five. Liz, you and I are on meet and greet together – Cole you're in the library and Taylor and Marcus have to be in the head's office with Patel and Lucas for any questions about what it's like being head boy and girl, blah, blah, blah..."

"Wait a sec," I interrupt, "does that mean Emily will be in the office, too? Cole, are you in there at any point?"

"Not that I know of." He looks worried, like he's dropped the ball. "Am I?"

"You should be for a bit, I think. Deputies normally stop in to say hello towards the end of the evening. She should be stationed somewhere, like you'll be at the library. Out of the way. Marcus can come and get you when I have to go for Emily," Taylor replies. She keeps glancing into a small, handheld mirror. The sore on her face looks red and angry now, even under the make-up. She winces. "I can't believe I have to woo prospective students looking like this."

"You still look great, babe," Marcus tries, but it's hard to agree. Taylor's usually bright skin is dull and her smile doesn't reach her eyes. You can tell she is in pain.

"OK," Kat continues, directing our attention back to

the scrap of paper. "Great, Emily will hopefully be out of the way, then. So, Liz, your first tour is at six, right?" I nod. "So is mine. They're meant to be half an hour, so we can meet in the foyer at six thirty. Cole, you're going to rock up at the office around half six and declare some kind of emergency in the library that Patel will need to attend..."

"Er, some kind of emergency?" Cole's voice vibrates through my back. "What am I going to say?"

"I dunno." Kat waves a hand airily. "You'll think of something. So – you'll all run to the library or wherever. Marcus and Tay, when Patel realizes nothing has happened, you just need to make sure she stays out of the way for a few minutes – the parents should be in the foyer, use them to distract her if you need to. One of you will have to wedge something in the office door—"

"I'll do that on the way out," Marcus volunteers with a salute.

"And Liz and I will slide on in from the hallway and start digging around."

"How do we know when she'll be coming back?" I ask anxiously, running the plan over in my brain. All the millions of things that could go wrong are dancing before my eyes. "If we get caught we'll be expelled," I whisper.

Quiet again. In spite of everything that has happened, none of us want to leave Morton.

"I'll keep watch and call you," Taylor says. "I'll nip into

the bathroom, call your burner and just let it ring. You won't have to answer – I'll stash my phone in there now. When you feel yours vibrate, Liz, both of you get out of there. OK?"

"Best idea I can think of," Kat shrugs. "Thanks, Tay. What do you reckon, Lizzie?"

"Yeah, me too," I admit. I look up at Cole. "I hope this is worth it."

"It will be," Cole murmurs into my hair and I let myself relax. He's right: it will be worth it. It will.

It has to be. I finish my tea and slide further back into him.

"I'd like this year to settle down already," he murmurs. "Think of all the time we could spend together if things were nice and boring."

"Hmm," I agree, enjoying the feel of his strong arms around me. "I miss boredom."

"All right, you two." Marcus threatens to spray us with his bottle of water. "That's enough now. Liz, I didn't think I'd ever have to say that to you." He gives me a wicked grin. "Not quite the good girl we all thought, are you?"

"Sorry," Cole and I both say, before grinning at each other.

"It's no good, Marcus." Taylor pulls herself away from the mirror, winking at me. "We've lost them."

"Come on, lovers, let's get ready." Kat stands up and straightens her uniform. Her usually wild hair is smoothed out, parted to one side. The dark ends curl around the lapels of her blazer and she is even wearing light make-up. "Ugh, I can't wait to put my leggings back on."

"You look great," I say to her before standing and turning to pull Cole out of his chair. "As do you." I readjust his collar that really doesn't need readjusting and let my hand linger on his broad chest for a second. It's a good job we're not stationed together this evening. He would be *far* too distracting. The thought takes me by surprise.

"You guys ready?" I ask Taylor and Marcus. Tay has managed to arrange her hair in a clever braid across the front of her hairline, almost like a headband. She has fluffed and teased the ends of it and, along with a deep part on the opposite side, it covers the majority of her wound. "Hey, good job."

"Thanks," she mutters, touching her cheek self-consciously. "It'll have to do for now. I'm going to have to sort this, though. I can't handle it any more. Right," she says a little louder, "I'm going to stash my phone. We'll see you guys later, when all this is done."

Marcus grabs her outstretched hand and follows her out to the corridor. "Upstairs? Just after eight?" He calls over his shoulder.

"Yeah." I nod, taking a deep breath. "See you then."

I've never given tours before and my palms are damp as

Kat and I walk to the main entrance. Dr Patel is already there, dressed in a crimson red trouser suit paired with glossy black heels and a slick of red lipstick. Her dark hair is shining and she's rocking the most accurate eyeliner flicks I've ever seen. Dangerous or not, the woman has got impeccable style.

She eyes us as we approach, all while giving out clipped orders and ushering people into position. I stand just inside the huge, open double doors and soak in the late evening sun. Uncomfortable cramps clutch at my stomach again.

Kat heads outside to greet cars as I try to discreetly rub my stomach. She looks shiny and polished too and I feel like an interloper for a moment. However well-turned-out I might look on the outside, I'll never feel that way on the inside. Another thing the shrink had me working on over the summer. *Self-worth*. I chant the little mantra she taught me internally to the rhythm of my hand circling my stomach: *I deserve to belong. I deserve to belong. I. Deserve. To. Belong.*

Better.

I take a deep breath through my nose and out through my mouth, refocusing my attention just in time to see the first car approach, its backdrop the quickly fading sky. The nights are getting darker now, waiting for the clocks to turn back on themselves.

I plaster on a smile as the first family reach the doors. "Welcome," I say, "to Morton Academy."

*

It turns out I'm actually quite good at this. I don't have to look at my notes once as I guide my first tour around – I have a head for dates and facts. I pause at the doors to each classroom and allow the prospective students to wander at their leisure, asking their questions to the prefects and staff stationed in each faculty so they can go away and settle on their two additional classes.

The cramps, though, are getting worse. I glance at the time and see we have fifteen minutes before Cole does – well, whatever he's going to do to create a distraction. I bite my lip as pain shoots through my abdomen. *Deep breaths, Liz. Ignore it.*

I spot a ladder over in the corner, near the top of the stairs. It was clearly used to hang the large welcome banner over the stained-glass window earlier today and no one has put it back. Patel will lose it if she sees it; everything was supposed to be picture perfect and this is covered in white splashes of paint. I glance into the room and see my charges are busy, so I make the decision to move the ladder. As I step towards it, I spot Emily coming up the stairs. *Damn.* I thought she'd be busy somewhere. She is the last thing we need.

I move the ladder carefully out of sight, away from the long draping lines that hold the banner up on brackets high above my head and race back to my station, hoping Emily doesn't decide now is a good time to collar me.

"Excuse me, Erin, Mr and Mrs Walker?" The family I'm guiding around gravitate back towards me. "I'd like to show you the ground floor now," I say. "Once our tour is over, you can view the whole of the school at your leisure." I give them what I hope is a winning smile. "Please, follow me."

We head back to the main staircase and begin our descent when I realize Emily is still there, her eyes fixed on the banner high above us. She still doesn't look well, the circles under her eyes evident even beneath the foundation she's caked on. She's washed her hair at least, but that eye is still twitching. She is not making a good impression.

"Er, excuse us, please, Emily," I say politely, guiding the Walker family around her. Erin, the prospective student, follows her gaze.

"Oh, look," Erin says softly, "the banner's coming down."

"So it is," I laugh merrily, continuing down the steps. "Trust Emily to spot that! She is our deputy head girl. I suppose she has an eye for when things aren't perfect."

Emily looks at me coldly and calls over, "Fix it."

I blink. What? "I'm on a tour with the Walkers," I say through gritted teeth, gesturing to the family. There's no way I'm getting on that ladder. I don't do heights. "I'll mention it to Mr Loomis once we're finished."

Emily rolls her eyes. "You are worse than useless,"

she mutters as the Walkers exchange glances and my smile cements itself in place. "Fine, I'll do *this* myself, too."

"Let's carry on, shall we?" I trill, as the Walkers continue to watch Emily climb up the stairs.

"She's not really going to try to get up there herself, is she?" Mr Walker, a watery man in glasses asks, rubbing the thinning patch on top of his head.

"No, of course not. She meant she was going to find the groundskeeper." At least I *think* that was what Emily meant.

We arrive at the bottom of the staircase and I try to distract them, pointing out the keystone that sits above the main doors. It's carved with the date 1838, the year the building was constructed.

"Please, after you." I gesture down the hallway and begin to escort the Walkers away from the bottom of the stairs. I don't want to go too far, as Cole will be here any second to distract Dr Patel. I am showing them a small map of the grounds, when a scream rips through the air.

It doesn't happen in slow-motion, like I might have thought. No, when a body drops through the air from that height it's fast, a sickening thunderclap, the visceral slap of flesh on stone.

I jerk my head up, even though it has already happened. The ladder hangs precariously over the uppermost part of the balcony, the banner still drooping idly at one corner, its ribbons hanging free from their mooring.

Silence rings in my ears as I turn to face the Walkers. Their faces are drained of colour, mouths open in horror as they stare at their daughter.

Erin stands frozen still, dotted with red splashes from head to toe, a pool of Emily's blood spreading at her feet.

35

Stupid girl.

She was so predictable. Another Little Miss Perfect. I knew when I saw her leave her station that if I loosened that banner her perfectionism would kick in. She would have to fix it herself, something she could be praised for.

Such a sycophant.

Shame I'd covered the ladder rungs in grease before she got to it. She wouldn't have had a chance – once she got up a few steps either her hands were going to go or her feet were. If I was lucky, both.

It appears I am incredibly *lucky, which was a shame for Emily.*

I suppose.

Now everything kicks into slow motion.

Hands guide me away from the bottom of the staircase and I follow blindly, barely registering as Dr Patel hurries the families away from the scene. My ears feel as though they are stuffed full of cotton wool so the cries of horror are muffled, but I do get a glimpse of Emily's blank, staring eyes. The huge pool of blood. One of the PE teachers, Mr Coffey, kneeling on the cold stone floor, her limp wrist in his hand. His slow head shake.

"She's dead," I mutter, the hands still strong around my arms as I realize I'm being steered towards Dr Patel's office. I turn my head, dazed. "Kat?"

"Sssh." She pushes me through the open door and shuts it gently behind us. "I know it's sick, but now's our chance. Jesus, Liz, I know we told Cole to create a distraction, but. . ."

"Cole didn't do this!" I gasp. "How could you even think that? I saw her, on the stairs, she tried to climb that ladder and . . . I think she was trying to fix the banner."

"Christ. Why would she do that?"

I shrug. "I don't know – she didn't look right."

"Christ," Kat repeats. "Right, well, we need to use it to our advantage. Get searching, look for anything that refers to the cult or to Patel's brother. There's got to be some kind of link in here."

"OK," I say, but my body is rooted to the spot. I search the room desperately, my eyes feeling like the ligaments that hold them in place are loosening, blurring everything at the edges. I raise a hand to my face to find my cheeks are wet and pull it away, expecting to see tears, but my fingers come away red and bile rises from my aching stomach.

"Come on," Kat hisses, already flipping through a filing cabinet. "Argh, these are useless, just our files." She pulls out a sepia brown folder. "Jeez, yours is big, Liz."

"All the medical stuff," I murmur, touching my head unconsciously. "You wouldn't believe the amount of appointments I had to have this summer."

"I bet." Kat smiles in sympathy and places the folder back. I head to the far side of the room and pull open the double doors of a floor to ceiling closet that's built into the walls.

"Can you believe she keeps this stuff unlocked?"

"I guess she usually locks the office door. Anything?" Kat doesn't look over, and carries on digging through the filing cabinet. How can she be so calm, so focused?

"I don't think so. . ." I scan lines of box files that blur together in uniformly neat, colour-coded rows. I read the labels. *Whistleblowing Policy, Staff Social Media Regulations, Curriculum Standards.* A couple of spare jackets and a formal dress gown hang underneath and a large umbrella and a pair of flats sits at the bottom. "Nothing," I say as I part the jackets to peer into the back. A sudden, searing cramp has me doubled over and I gasp in pain.

"Are you OK? Don't think about what just happened, just . . . lock it away. Deal with it later. Liz?"

"Yeah." I clench my jaw against the pain as my muscles spasm. Emily's crumpled body lying on the ground flashes into my mind. My throat is full of needles as my muscles spasm.

"Is it your stomach again?" Kat crosses the room to join me.

"Yeah." I take a deep breath, forcing the image of Emily from my mind. The pain recedes. "Ouch."

"You think it's something you've eaten? Or . . . drunk?"

My mind flashes back to Cole handing me a mug of Earl Grey.

"No. Maybe. I just need to . . . ignore it." I pant. I drag out a large, worn box from the cupboard, more in an effort to distract myself than anything. "This looks promising."

It's pretty, made from smooth, polished wood and inlaid with patterns in what looks like mother of pearl. It's clean, too, not dusty as I expected. Like it's been opened recently. "How long have we been in here?" I ask, as I ease the lid off.

"Not even five minutes, but we need to be quick."

"OK." We peer at the contents. Photos, mainly. Some folded letters on lined paper with ragged edges, as if torn from an exercise book. They have clearly been read and refolded many times, some in the original envelopes, complete with yellowed gum and ancient stamps. "Is it a memory box?"

"I guess so." Kat pulls out a Polaroid photograph. The white border has the faded words, "Minahil's wedding, Goa, 1996" written on it in marker pen and the picture shows a family of four dressed in the most beautiful Indian wedding outfits. Two proud parents stand behind a boy and girl, all four of them beaming. One of the kids is obviously Dr Patel. 1996 would make her twelve or thirteen, I suppose, but she was already prettier than most girls her age. Smarter, too, if she ended up being head girl here.

I study the picture carefully. Her brother looks slightly older, maybe fourteen or so, and he has a self-assured, almost cocky aura around him.

"It really was him last night," Kat breathes, "I didn't quite believe it."

"It's kind of sad, isn't it? They all looked so happy," I whisper, thinking back to the newspaper articles as Kat replaces the photograph. I thumb through the rest of the contents, finding more family photos and even some of Dr Patel and some other kids in Morton uniforms, all looking nineties fabulous in their brown lipliner and skinny eyebrows. The boys have their hair parted in curtains. "Wait, what's this?"

Right at the bottom of the box there's another small, thick envelope addressed to Nikhita Patel. But the postmark is recent. Like, this year recent. I pull out the thickly wadded paper, pages and pages of scribbled handwriting, and my eyes widen. It's from her brother. "Oh, my God. Kat. We were right." I thrust the letter towards her and she scans it.

"Harrison's out?"

"Looks like it." I glance through the other pages. One shows a printed image of a small, terracotta angel. It stares back at me, its face blank, barely sculpted. It is the Bernini I showed Cole. *My* Bernini.

"Is that the angel from the library?" Kat asks, plucking the page from my hand. "Weird."

"Is it?" My mind is whirring, trying to put the pieces together. "So, we have a letter from Patel's brother saying that Harrison is out of prison. and it sounds like her brother and Harrison stayed in touch, all these years."

"Which is creepy as, considering what they were both in jail for."

"Very," I agree. "But now *he's* out and her *brother* suddenly shows up. Even though he did time for her attempted murder? Dr Patel clearly has no problem meeting with Rikesh. What if she's actually trying to help him? Help both of them?"

"You think Patel is actually part of the cult? And the deaths here are all sacrifices, like they before?"

"It's a theory." I tap the printout of the Bernini. "But what does this have to do with it all?"

"I don't kn—" Kat is interrupted by the sound of the door handle. We stare at each other with wide eyes, then jam the lid back on the box and shove it in the cupboard, closing it just as the door swings open. I shove the printout of the Bernini into my waistband.

Kat drags me into a hug and strokes my hair. "Follow my lead?" she whispers. Then, more loudly, "Shush, Lizzie, it's OK, Dr Patel will be here soon and everything will be fine."

A throat clears. "What are you doing in here, girls?"

"Oh, Dr Patel!" Kat releases me as I make a show of wiping my now-dry face. "Dr Patel, we were so scared!" The headmistress has kept her composure but her pale face and shaking hands give her away. "We didn't know where to go after ... after Emily..."

"You were there?" she asks softly. "When she fell?"

249

We nod and I look down at the floor, unable to meet her eye. There are dull splatters on my polished shoes and bile rises in my throat when I realize what it is.

"Oh God," I whisper. "I need to shower." Patel and Kat's eyes both travel down to my shoes and the reddish-brown splashes across the front of my white socks. My throat heaves and I clap a hand over my mouth.

"You should see the nurse," Patel says kindly. Well, kindly for her, anyway. I shake my head. "Fine, then. Off to bed, both of you. The school grounds are on lockdown until tomorrow at the very earliest – that means you do not leave your rooms, except to use the facilities or come to assembly tomorrow morning. I have sent the head boy and girl to communicate this to the rest of the students. Do you understand?"

We nod mutely. Lockdown. I scramble to think what this means. How this feeds into Patel's plan, if she really is behind all of this.

"Er, Dr Patel?" Kat says. "There's something we think you should know." I stare at her, wondering what the hell she's playing at.

"Go on," says Dr Patel.

"We saw a stranger on the grounds at the open evening. But he wasn't with anyone. About this tall" – she holds up her hand – "and Indian descent, I think."

"Thank you for letting me know, Ms Paphitis." Is it just me or is Dr Patel's pristine make-up now shadowed with grey? "We have had a lot of journalists snooping around recently. I will alert the faculty."

"Oh. Thank you." Kat leads the way to the door and I follow in a daze as Dr Patel walks around to sit at her desk. As I start to move, a wadded-up piece of paper flutters to the floor.

The Bernini.

I snatch it back up and shove it into my pocket, but not before I see Dr Patel's face, her eyes burning a hole into my pocket.

"She's definitely rattled." Kat shuts the door behind her and leans on it briefly. We're both shaking. "Do you think she saw the picture, when you dropped it?"

"I don't know." We are in the storeroom to use the back staircase – I don't think we'll use the main one again for a while. "I hope not."

"Same," she mutters. She pulls the door open and gestures for me to lead the way. "Well, Lizzie," she jokes, "I didn't think I'd ever be in here with you."

"Hilarious," I say forlornly, thinking of Cole. "Do you think the others are still waiting for us?"

"I dunno." She glides past me, climbing the steps two at a time as I pant behind her. "Do you wanna check?"

"Yeah, I guess." I think of the mess on my shoes. "I really do need a shower, though."

"Ditto." She pushes the door at the top and we emerge

into the tiny cleaning closet. "Come on, let's go and find them first, then showers."

We walk the long way around the first floor in silence, past darkened classrooms, avoiding the main staircase again. There are no sirens, but red and blue lights wash over the walls of each teaching space we pass. The police are definitely here. There's a slight chatter of people, those guarding the scene and the final few outsiders being questioned. The Walkers are probably still here. Otherwise, the building is silent. Holding its breath. Dr Patel wasn't joking when she said the place was locked down. She must have kicked out every family that wasn't in the foyer on the spot. God knows how she's going to keep this one quiet, with members of the public here when it happened.

When we finally reach our corridor, all of the doors are open and girls are wandering in and out of each other's rooms, some red-faced and bawling, others drained of colour. One of the girls from Kat's English class passes us and Kat stops her. "Hey, Beck, have you seen Taylor?"

"No, sorry." Her eyes widen as she clocks me, the specks of blood on my face and neck. "Oh my God, you were there, weren't you? Are you OK?"

"Thanks, Beck." Kat dismisses her and we carry on. Our door is closed and we peek in, hoping to see Taylor, but the room is empty.

"Upstairs?" I say.

"Yeah, she must be." We head to the spiral staircase

and climb up, both unconsciously tiptoeing, as though we don't want to disturb anyone.

"Nobody here," Kat announces, as she reaches the top. The lounge is completely empty. "Lockdown must be pretty serious. Let's try her room."

The door is shut. I knock but there's no answer so I try the handle and it opens easily. The bedroom is empty and the en-suite door is shut. "Tay?" I call.

"Don't come in!" Taylor's voice sounds panicked through the wooden door. "I'm fine!"

Kat and I look at each other. "She doesn't sound fine," I say. Kat nods in agreement.

"Taylor, honey?" Kat inches towards the door and presses herself to it. "Is everything OK?"

"Yes!" Taylor's answer verges on a squeal and Kat looks at me wide-eyed, shocked by the hysterical edge to her voice. I shake my head. She is definitely not.

"Taylor, babe, I'm coming in. I just want to check you're safe." Kat wraps one hand around the doorknob, ready to turn.

"No, no, don't come in." Taylor's voice is too fast, breathless. "It's OK, I'm fine, honestly. I'm fine, I'm fine, I'm fine. . ."

"You don't sound fine," I say loudly. No response.

"Tay, don't make me open the lock from out here. It's only one of those stupid turn locks, not like the dorm doors. I could open it with a coin."

"I don't want anyone to see me," Taylor wails from the bathroom. I take a deep breath.

"Taylor," I try, "did something happen to you? You can tell us, we can help."

There's a pause, then a click from the other side of the door as Taylor turns the lock. Progress. I nod at Kat and she grabs the handle with a shaking hand and pushes open the door.

Taylor is standing there in a white towel, facing away from us. Her red hair is wet, almost black, hanging down her back in thick ropes.

"Taylor?" I try again.

She starts to shuffle around slowly, her breath coming in ragged little gasps and I hold my breath. Her head is bowed, as though she's praying, and strings of hair cover her face. She starts to raise her head slowly, making tortured little animal noises as she does. "I tried to fix it," she sobs, "I just tried to fix it." She lifts her head up and pushes the hair behind her ears.

"Oh my God," Kat gasps and Taylor starts to wail.

"I just, it was so sore, the pressure was too much, so I started to squeeze and all this green pus started to come out and then ... then this..." She breaks into sobs again as I study the gaping wound on her face. It's blackened at the edges, like the flesh is rotting, eating her face from the inside out. "I don't know what to do!" she cries, taking deep breaths between each word. Kat races towards her to give her a hug when the smell hits me. The wound has been festering, all right, and the air is thick with the smell of sickness, infection. I see that this close up, there is a flash of white inside the gash.

I can't help but think it's her bone.

37

Looks like I'm going to have to do something about that nosy bitch. She keeps opening her big mouth, getting herself involved.

If I'm not careful, she's going to uncover exactly what I'm planning to do.

I keep thinking about the memory box, the one with all of those letters and photographs in it. The family photo is the most condemning thing, I think, along with the letter from Rikesh – I'll have to think about what to do with those. They need to stay in the right hands. Mine, preferably.

I have time now, though. Lockdown will probably continue until the end of the weekend at least, the police on duty are paid

off and everyone else is confined to their quarters, staff included.
That gives me three days to pull this off.

I know I can do it.
It's time to finally get what I deserve.

38

"I think you should stay in bed." I stroke Taylor's hair as I perch on the edge of her bed, the one in our room, trying to soothe her back to sleep. Her cheek looks slightly better after she let us clean and dress it for her, but the ends are still puckered beneath the Steri-Strips that are holding her face together, the skin swollen and purple in the morning light.

"No." She tries to push herself up but retches as soon as she's in a sitting position. "I'm head girl, I have to be at assembly. Especially after yesterday. Please?"

"No." I help her shaking form back down on to the pillows and study her face. "Are you sure you don't want to see the nurse, Tay?"

"No, no, it's fine. She'll just want to put me on fluids and I don't even want to think about needles. I'll drink loads of water, I promise. Do you have any more painkillers, though?"

"Here." Kat pulls a blister packet from her bedside drawer. "It's an anti-inflammatory, it should take the swelling down." We watch as Taylor chokes them down with a glass of water before retching again.

"Fine," she says sleepily. "I'll stay in bed. But you tell me everything when you get back."

"Of course," I say, as Kat continues to search her drawer. "What are you looking for?"

"My Tiger Balm, my neck is killing me. Have you seen it?"

"No, but here." I dig into my pockets for one I found in the bathroom the other day. "I found this one."

"Thank you." She grabs the little tub and twists the golden lid off, rubbing the greasy liquid into the nape of her neck.

"Hmmmm," Taylor says sleepily, her words barely strung together. "I love that smell, smells like Marcus. I could just eat it."

"Yeah, you don't wanna do that," Kat laughs. "It's totally toxic. I think like a spoonful can kill you."

"No way," Taylor says through a yawn, half engulfed in sleep. "Hmmm." Kat and I watch as Taylor's eyes finally flicker to a close and she settles down.

"Come on," I whisper to Kat as I shrug on my blazer. "Let's leave her to it. Should we lock the door?"

Kat thinks for a minute. "Yeah," she decides. "I'll slide my key under so she can get out if she needs to. It's hard to trust anyone at the moment, isn't it?"

She turns the key with a click. Her words ring in the air.

The atmosphere in assembly is fraught. Assemblies usually take place on Mondays, Wednesdays and Fridays, so this *shouldn't* be any different, being a Friday morning, but of course it is. The ghosts of Morgan, Jameela, Frank and Emily stalk the edges of the hall as students whisper to one another, conspiracy theories trickling down their neat lines. Silence quickly descends as Dr Patel enters the hall, her spiked heels practically sparking off the stone floor, followed by the other senior staff. They climb the steps to the stage in a solemn procession and stand in a line behind the headmistress.

"Good morning." Dr Patel speaks into the microphone, her voice calm, measured. "I will not keep you here for long – I will come straight to the point of today's assembly. As you will all know, there was a most unfortunate accident last night at open evening. It is my sad duty to tell you that Emily Sinclair, our deputy head girl, passed away immediately following the incident." The hall instantly fills with muted chatter, especially from the juniors, who hadn't taken part in the event last night. Dr Patel raises one hand and the whispers cease. "You will notice a police

260

presence around the building. All of the proper procedures have been put in place, which means that as of last night, Morton Academy is in emergency lockdown. No one leaves the grounds and no one enters them, either."

"Liar," Kat hisses.

"I trust that you will follow the rules during this period. Classes have been suspended for today and the main staircase is out of bounds. You may use the back staircases or disabled elevator. Once you return upstairs, you will be expected to stay on the second and third floors, in your dorms or the appropriate lounges. Do you understand?"

A chorus of shocked agreement ripples around the hall.

"Excuse me, Dr Patel?" My skin shrinks as Kat raises her hand – and voice – above the crowd.

The crowd falls silent.

"Yes?" Dr Patel raises her perfectly groomed eyebrows while her lips tighten.

"Why exactly are we in lockdown? If Emily's death was an accident."

Dr Patel sighs into the microphone. "Because, Ms Paphitis, we do not believe it *was* an accident. We believe Emily was pushed."

The hall empties out in shocked silence and I scan the crowd for Marcus and Cole. "There," I say, grabbing Kat's hand and bumping through the crowd to intercept them at the door.

"Hey," I call, as quietly as I can. Cole's head whips around to the sound of my voice and I feel an ill-timed flush of pleasure. He grabs Marcus's arm and points out to the hallway. We follow them, detaching from the rest of the crowd who are heading to the back staircase. Cole drags me into a hug immediately and we allow the crowd to disperse around us.

"Thank God you're not hurt," he breathes into my hair. I squeeze him as tight as I can.

"Hey." Marcus narrows his eyes as we release each other. "Where's Taylor?"

"She's in bed." I wince as I think of her face last night. "She didn't text you this morning?"

"No. She didn't reply last night, either. I just thought she was in shock or something. Is she ill?"

Kat and I glance at each other, clearly thinking the same thing – why didn't he just come and see her? We might be in separate dorms but that hadn't bothered him the other night, when he flaunted the rules by coming up to the girls' lounge.

"No," Kat says slowly. "I'm not sure if she is." She explains the scene we walked in on in the bathroom last night. "We left her in bed to rest, but honestly? I think she needs to see the nurse."

"I'm going up to see her." Marcus's jaw is tight. "It could be sepsis. God, why didn't I notice? Was she sick?"

"No," I say, "but she did feel sick earlier. She was retching this morning, even after water."

"And does the wound smell?"

"Yes," I admit, nervous now. "It did last night. But, Marcus, she's a clever girl, she knows about this stuff, doesn't she? If she was worried. . ."

"You don't understand." He cuts me off. "Taylor is exhausted. She didn't want anyone to know, but she's on the verge of failing her classes. She's been studying at all hours and when I followed her out of the library the other day, she just broke down. There's no way she'd take time off to go to the nurse. She's anxious and exhausted and her immune system will be useless because of it. And I haven't helped. . ."

He shakes his head, leaving the sentence hanging, and starts towards the storeroom.

We follow him up, through the first-floor corridors and up to the senior girls' dorm rooms, silent and breathless. What if Taylor really is that sick? We arrive in our corridor and I am suddenly breathless. I stop a minute and lean against the wall. Cole pauses with me.

"You OK?" He holds a hand out to me. I grab it gratefully and he takes my weight as I straighten up.

"Yeah, I think so."

"Is it true — were you there? When Emily. . ." He narrows sad brown eyes at me and I remember what a horrible start he's had here.

I nod and look down towards our room. I don't know if I'm OK or not.

Kat and Marcus approach our door further down the corridor. We hover behind them.

"Liz, have you got the key?"

"What? No, I thought you did?"

"No, I slid mine back under, remember? Oh, God, we've locked her in!" Kat wrenches the handle but the door is locked firmly. Her voice begins to rise as panic grips her. "Taylor?" she shouts, pressing her face up to the door. "Taylor!" she tries again, banging. She turns to me with desperate eyes. "Liz, are you sure you don't have a key?"

"I'm sure," I whisper, so quietly I'm not sure she hears me. I watch as she hammers on the door, unable to do anything. It's like I'm frozen to the spot.

"Move," Marcus growls. Kat takes one look at his face and does as he says. "These doors are useless, one of the seniors last year managed to deck one in." He eyes the wood, searching for weak points.

"It's a fire door," I croak, finding my voice. "Some of them are hollow. You might be able to break through it."

We move back in unison, giving Marcus space as he bounces up and down on the balls of his feet. "Right." He drops his centre of gravity and launches himself at the door, using his shoulder, aiming for the centre. He pulls away and there's a faint depression in the middle.

"Yes, it's hollow. Keep going," Kat urges. "You can do this."

Marcus steps back and runs a hand over his hair before launching himself again. This time there's an audible crack and it seems to spur him on. He throws himself at it over and over again, the wood veneer splintering beneath his shoulders. When there's a fist-sized hole in the middle, he fires instructions at Kat and the two of them start kicking out bits of wood until there's a space large enough for Marcus to squeeze through. I hang back, shoving my hands into my blazer pockets, unsure of what to do. My hand closes around something cool and the blood drains from my face. *My key.*

Kat ducks to look through the door and I gently withdraw my hand.

"Oh, God, oh Taylor, no!" Kat throws herself through the opening and fumbles around on the floor, retrieving the key and unlocking what's left of the door for us. I trail slowly behind Cole.

"Taylor?" I whisper. She's lying in the bed where we left her, but her eyes are shut and her mouth is crusted with vomit. The room smells putrid, like something has. . .

"No, no," Marcus's keening cry needles into my ears. "Taylor, Tay, baby, come on. Please, I'm sorry, I'm sorry." He goes to pull her up into his arms but Cole stops him.

"Marcus, mate, stop. Marcus!" He turns wild eyes on Cole. "Come on, remember what we've got to do. Recovery position, all that stuff."

"I can't." His voice catches. "I don't remember. . ."

"Well, I do." He holds a hand over Taylor's mouth and nose. "Shit, she's not breathing. Kat, go and ring down for the nurse, you can do that on the phone in the hallway, right?"

"Yes, right." Kat leaves the room on autopilot and I shrink back into the wall, letting Cole take control of the situation.

"Marcus, trust me. Give me some space. Liz, can you get some water?" I nod as I grab a half-drunk bottle from the side table, not taking my eyes off him as he gently lowers Taylor from the bed to the floor. Her arms flop uselessly and her skin is grey against her shock of red hair. He goes through the motions as Marcus paces behind him, bending her knee and rolling her over. He tilts her head back to open her windpipe and waits a second for her to start breathing again.

Nothing. Cole looks at me with huge eyes, his assurance fading. Marcus paces behind him with his face in his hands.

"Clear her throat," I remember, though I can barely hear myself. "Clear her throat," I repeat.

"Yes." Cole nods and opens Taylor's mouth, checking for any foreign objects. I squeeze my eyes shut as he forces his fingers into her throat.

Still, nothing.

"The nurses are on their way." I peel open my eyes at Kat's voice, just as Cole is about to roll Taylor on to her back, psyching himself up for CPR. "Oh, God. Oh, Taylor," Kat groans, sinking to the floor, clutching the doorframe so hard her knuckles are white. We can do nothing other than watch in mute horror as Cole pinches her nose between his thumb and forefinger and expels two deep breaths into her, her chest rising and falling. He leans back on his heels and starts chest compressions that I count silently along with him.

The only sound in the room now is the faint cracking of Taylor's ribs and Marcus's sobs.

"Come on, Taylor," Cole growls before leaning down and pumping two more breaths into her. He starts compressions again. One-two-three-four—

Taylor's eyes pop open.

"Cole!" I scream and he stops, his eyes wide with shock. Taylor starts to gasp for breath, her windpipe rattling as he quickly turns her back on her side so she can cough up the vomit that was clogging her lungs.

"Taylor?" Marcus drops to his knees behind Cole, tears streaming openly down his face. "Oh, Taylor, thank you, thank you. . ."

Cole moves out of the way to let Marcus sit by her, but stays close, rubbing her back as she coughs up the last of it. I hand him the water and he pours some into her mouth but it filters straight out again as Taylor's eyes roll back in her head.

"No!" Marcus screams, as Cole grabs her wrist.

"Mate, it's OK, it's OK. Her pulse is strong, she's

just unconscious."

"Jesus, we have to get her help right now." Marcus scoops her up from the floor as though she's nothing but a ragdoll. She looks dead, the way she is hanging there, limp in his arms. One of her pyjama legs is pushed up to her knee and I have a crazy need to push it down, so she's not embarrassed when people see her.

"The nurse is on her way," Kat tries again, louder this time, but Marcus steps over her and starts to carry his girlfriend down the hallway, her head bobbing with each huge stride, as the three of us stand uselessly in the shattered doorway.

39

I pour a splash of milk into the dark cup of tea on the counter, watching it swirl as I add a heaped spoon of sugar and stir. I balance it on a saucer, my hands still shaking, and head back to where I left Cole, on the sofa closest to Taylor's room in the senior lounge. As usual, it's deserted – everyone else must be in the corridor still. We had left practically the whole of the senior girls gawping at the hole in our bedroom door after Marcus left, Kat sprinting behind them.

"Here." I place the cup down in front of Cole. His colour is starting to come back but his hands are still shaking and his eyes are unfocused. "Here," I waffle, pointing to the cup. "You're in shock. You need some sugar in your system, a police officer once taught me that."

He nods, puppet-like.

I sit down, careful not to crowd him, but I do reach across to take his hand. "What you did back there was amazing, you know that, right?"

"I thought. . . I thought she was. . ."

"I know," I soothe, moving closer and pushing a lock of hair behind his ear. "I know. We all did. But she's not, because of you." He grips my hand for a second and releases it, reaching for the cup instead. He takes a gulp, even though it must be scalding, and his eyes clear a little.

"That is good, thanks." We sit in silence as he drains the tiny cup.

"Do you want another? I'd have done you a mug but it's hidden downstairs."

"Behind the fireplace in the common room. I know." He smiles. "No, I'm fine. I could sleep for a week though."

"Do it, then. Here." I edge to the corner of the sofa and balance a threadbare cushion on my lap. "Lie down."

"You sure? Do you think they're OK?" he says weakly.

"Yes. Kat texted me and said she'd come back as soon as she had news. It's been less than half an hour. You need to relax, that was a massive thing you just did." He nods, finishes the tea, and leans back, gently placing his head in my lap, his long legs stretched out along the sofa. We're both still in our uniforms, which seems absurd, and he tugs his tie loose, undoes his top button. He closes his eyes as I fight the impulse to stroke his perfect face or trail my fingers along the dip of his throat.

"Thanks for looking after me," he whispers, raising my hand to his lips and kissing the back of it.

"Of course," I whisper back, watching as his breath starts to settle, his chest rising and falling. I envy his ability to fall asleep like that; I haven't been able to do it since the accident. I give in to my urges and trace one finger across the arches of his upper lip. It's a perfect cupid's bow, mesmerizing. His nose twitches and I pull my hand away, but he grabs it back sleepily and places it on his cheek.

"Keep going," he mutters.

I gently run my fingers across his cheek before moving my hands up to his hair, combing my fingers through, using my nails to trace little circles as his body relaxes even more deeply into mine. I don't know how long I watch him sleep for, but the next thing I know, a hand is gently shaking my shoulder.

"Hey." Kat edges around the sofa and perches on an armchair. "How is he?"

I rub my blurry eyes and glance down at Cole, who is still breathing deeply. "He's tired. I must have nodded off too. So, how is she?"

"Should we wake him up?"

I really don't want to, he looks so peaceful, but she obviously wants to tell us something together. "Yeah, I guess so. Cole?" I brush the hair from his forehead and give his shoulder a little shake. "Hey, Cole, Kat's here. Wake up." He starts to blink and lets out a huge yawn. Kat stifles one too as she watches him. "Kat?" he repeats, his voice thick with sleep. "Kat!" He sits bolt upright so fast it makes me jump. "Sorry, sorry, Liz." He pats my leg. "Kat – how is Taylor?" He grabs hold of my hand as we both stare at Kat expectantly.

"She's OK." Cole lets out a sigh of relief that's half sob and half laugh and I squeeze his hand. "Well, she's not, but she's alive. Thanks to you."

"Oh, thank God." He pulls his hands from mine and presses his face into them. He stays that way for a second.

"Did they say what was wrong with her?" I ask.

"They think it is sepsis, like Marcus said." Kat shakes her head. "I can't believe I didn't realize, I mean she was so sick this morning."

"It's not your fault," I try, but my voice is quiet. "None of us did anything to help her, did we? We've all been too busy with . . . everything." The deaths of our classmates hang like spectres in the air between us. "Poor Taylor."

"How serious is it?" Cole asks.

"Pretty bad. She hadn't regained consciousness by the time the ambulance arrived, so. . ."

"Ambulance?" I butt in.

"Yeah. Nurse Templeton and Marcus went with her, I think someone called her parents, but they live so far

272

away... I didn't realize how bad sepsis could be – they had to get her to a hospital before her organs started to shut down."

"Jesus," I whisper. "When will we know more?"

"I dunno. I asked Marcus to text me when he knows more. Get this, though – Patel tried to stop them."

"What do you mean?"

"She tried to stop Marcus and the nurse calling an ambulance. Said we could deal with it here, that we were on lockdown, no one in, no one out, blah blah blah."

"Seriously?" I ask. "She said that? What the hell is she playing at?"

"I don't know, but whatever it is, she doesn't want anyone coming into the grounds right now."

"To the point where another student dies, though?" Cole asks, his face incredulous.

Kat leans forwards. "What if this lockdown, Emily's death – what if it's all a cover for something else, something bigger?"

"Like what, though?" I wonder aloud.

"I dunno," Kat admits. "Cult stuff? What if they bring Bradley Harrison in and just *kill* us all."

"Jesus, Kat, are you serious?" Cole stretches and shoots me a look.

"Yes," she answers, before shrugging. "No. Oh, I don't know. I don't have a clue what the hell is going on."

Cole gets to his feet. "In that case, I'm making more tea.

You guys want some?" We both nod as he glances sleepily around the room. "Where am I going?"

"Over there." I point to the patio doors. "There's a little kitchen around that corner."

"Thanks." We watch as he ambles off and almost immediately Kat's smile fades. She closes strong fingers around my wrist.

"I need to talk to you, now," she hisses, low so Cole can't hear her. My eyes drop to her iron grip.

"Kat, you're hurting me."

She loosens her hand. "Sorry. I'm just – I'm scared. I think I've figured something out and I don't want to say it, but. . ."

"Tell me." I glance towards the kitchen to make sure Cole is still there and hear the reassuring clank of cups being pulled from cupboards and the kettle starting its low hum.

"I've been thinking about all the people who have been ... hurt. I think that's where the connection is. I overheard Templeton talking about Emily with one of the coppers, while we were waiting for the ambulance. Emily's hands and the soles of her shoes were coated in something that smelled of menthol. Like Vicks. Or it could have been Tiger Balm I guess, they smell the same."

"What?"

"I know. If it was on her hands and feet, that meant it was on the rungs of the ladder. Someone put it there on

274

purpose, so the next person to use it would fall. You know, like they greased it. Pre-meditated."

"But how would they know it would be Emily using it next? Or that *anyone* else would touch it?"

"I dunno," she admits. "But I'm not finished. When I heard that, I went back to our room and checked the ingredients on the pot of Tiger Balm I have. Do you know what the main one is?"

"Camphor," I remember. "You told me that last night. It's poisonous, right?"

"Right. But nowadays most camphor is synthetic. The one used in Tiger Balm is. Do you know what the scientific name for synthetic camphor is?"

"No. Kat, where are you going with this?"

"It's trimethylbicyclo heptan." She stares at my blank face. "Remember? The chemical we found in Jameela's inhaler when we did the gas chromatography! The chemical that shouldn't have been there."

"What? How do you know that?"

"The pharmaceutical name is on the label. It was right under our noses the whole time, literally. Someone must have filled the mouthpiece of the inhaler with it and when Jameela started having an asthma attack, she must have sucked it right in. She practically ate the stuff. Her lungs were already under pressure – she didn't really have a chance."

"So it *was* murder," I whisper. "But what about Taylor?

The scratch on her face was because of a loose nail in her blusher brush. That can't have been deliberate, can it?"

"Maybe it was put there on purpose, I dunno." Kat shrugs as I glance over to see what's taking Cole so long. He's leaning on the kitchen counter, staring out of the window, the kettle sending up puffs of steam behind him. "I haven't had time to think about that yet. But look at the others." She starts ticking off dead girls on her fingers. "Morgan, drowned. Officially an accident. But she was an excellent swimmer, she nailed the records last year, she even set a new one for the hundred metres. We didn't think Patel was there but, honestly, most of us don't remember, do we? Next there was Jameela. Another tragic accident. Only not. And what did Jameela and Morgan have in common?"

"They were best friends," I say, "and so was Emily. They were all so tight, like they'd known each other for ever."

Kat shakes her head. "No – I mean, yeah, you're right, but think about what *else* they were. Head girl, Lizzie. They were all head girl, or were next in line to be."

I try to follow. "And you're saying Frank fits this pattern because he was deputy head boy?"

Kat frowns. "I don't think that's why Frank was killed. In fact, I'm not convinced his murder was planned, not like the others anyway."

"So. . ." She's on a roll and doesn't let me finish.

"They all had a huge future ahead of them, thanks to

Jewel and Bone. A future that Patel didn't get to have, because of her brother. He ruined things by snitching on Harrison. But now Harrison is out. Finally they can enact the sacrifice. Patel can achieve the success she always dreamed of – if she sacrifices everyone in line to be head girl this year..."

"Right," I agree, incredulous. "And Emily was deputy so she'd have been next..."

"After Tay, who was the new head girl..."

"Now there's hardly anyone left in the running, is there? Not really, I mean there's Ayesha, and Beck and Caroline, but they came after us in the hunt, so..." I say, reality dawning on me.

Kat nods. "No one else apart from us, and we're the ones sticking our noses in." She stares directly into my eyes. "What did that message on the mirror say? When you were in the shower room."

"*Dead girls can't win.*" I say it slowly, the words dripping from my mouth like poison. I start to shake. "What do we do now?" I ask.

"We need to stick together," says Kat firmly. "We're the new head and deputy, or will be, which means we're next on the list. We don't leave each other alone for a second. And we get all the evidence we can to prove Patel was involved. Deal?"

"Deal," I reply, realizing we have no other choice.

It's finally time.

The whole of Morton is on lockdown and no one is coming in or out for the foreseeable future. I made sure of that.

There are just a few things to do first. A few idiots who think it's a good idea to get in my way. And then I'll have it. Everything I want, everything I deserve. Everything I have dreamed about for so long.

Tonight, this ends.

41

"This wasn't what I had in mind when you said we should stick together."

It's Saturday morning, we're still in lockdown mode, the weather is glorious and the gym is empty. Plus, it smells: a combination of old sweat and lemon cleaning spray.

"Listen, it'll be good for you, I promise. If nothing it'll take your mind off Tay until we hear something." Kat pulls on a pair of grey weight gloves and, despite myself, I still look at her coordinated outfit with a touch of envy. Everything matches, from her cropped, mesh hoody to her brilliantly clean trainers. "Come on, you can spot me first. I'll show you what to do. I'll take it easy on you, promise."

"Yeah, right." I follow her over to the weights, a section of the gym I wouldn't dream of going to. I'd normally come in and have a half-hearted jog on the treadmill while Taylor does sprints, or maybe go on the bike so I could sit down. The weights section used to intimidate me.

Taylor. I wonder if she'll be OK.

"Let's try a simple bench press first." Kat talks me through how to push the weights on to the bar and secure them with clips at each end, before sliding herself beneath the barbell, one leg either side of the bench. "Right, you just stand over me and if I need help, you help me lift the barbell back on to the rack."

"I guess so." I stand behind her head, looking at her upside-down face beneath me. "Er, how much weight is on here?"

"Thirty kilos." She smiles. "Starting light."

"Light? That's almost half of me!"

"I can do a solid sixty-five but I have to warm up to it. Ready?" I nod, even though I know there's no way that I can lift thirty kilograms if she's in trouble.

Kat clasps her hands wide apart on the bar, wriggling her gloved fingers before finding her grip. She takes a deep breath and pushes her arms up, lifting the bar into the air. I step back and watch as she brings the barbell down to her chest and pushes back up, locking her elbows at the top.

"Kat, that's insane!" She grins at me through gritted teeth.

"Count," she puffs.

"Oh, right. Er, one." She keeps going like a machine until we reach ten and her arms wobble. I grab the bar and help guide it back on to the rack, feeling utterly useless as I do.

"Right." Kat stands up and takes a long gulp of water. "Your turn."

"There's no way I can do even one of those," I protest.

"Oh, don't worry – here." She starts to undo the clips and slides the plates off one side, so I copy her, removing the other. "We'll do it with no plates on. The bar weighs twenty on its own, so let's have a go at that." She smiles at me expectantly and I realize it's my turn to lie on the bench.

"I don't think I can," I say, my voice small.

"You won't know unless you try," she says encouragingly. "If you can't, I'll grab a lighter bar. Just give it a go. For me?" She turns big, brown puppy dog eyes on me.

"Fine, but you need to save me if anything goes wrong, deal?"

Kat laughs. "Deal."

I slip beneath the bar like I saw Kat do a few minutes ago and stare up at her.

"Ready?"

"No."

"You are. Here." She pats the bar. "Hands here, evenly spaced out but not too wide. You want to take a deep breath when you lower the bar and force it all out when you lift it back up. Ready now?"

"I guess so." The metal is cool against my sweaty palms, the crosshatched pattern on the bar etching into my skin. I wonder if that's why Kat wears gloves to do this. I hold on tight and push it up, Kat's hands guiding me. I feel a tightness around my ribs and back, every ligament and tendon pulled tight. God, it's heavy.

"I'm going to let go now, but I've got you." Kat says. I don't even try to respond. The tops of my arms start to burn and a band of muscle I was not even aware I had strains across my chest as I lower the bar. "Good, halfway there. Now, big breath out and push up, press your back into the bench if you need to, that's it! Push your feet into the floor..."

I follow her instructions as best as I can but it's like there's an invisible giant pushing down on me. I squeeze my eyes shut and push with all my strength. It's so heavy I'm worried I'll pop something, but it's as if a barrier breaks and suddenly my arms straighten up, elbows locking painfully.

Then relief, as the weight is taken from my hands.

"Lizzie, well done!" Kat squeals, replacing the bar as I pant up at her. "You did it!"

"Barely," I choke, pushing myself into a sitting position. "Jeez, how do you do that all the time?"

"Practice," she says, handing me my water bottle. I

take a deep swig and go to stand up, but blackness starts to crawl across my eyes, creeping in from the corners. I sit down again.

"Whoa," I say thickly. My ears are full of a high-pitched whine. "Woozy."

"Aww, no." Kat sits next to me and eases my head down between my knees, where I take several deep breaths, my vision clearing, darkness receding. "I'm sorry, I didn't think it'd mess with your head."

"It's OK." I wave a hand at her and take another swig of water before sitting up carefully. "I've been a bit off recently, anyway, with that bug or whatever it was that I had."

"Bug? You mean, those stomach cramps?"

"Yeah." I say. Kat looks uncomfortable. "What is it?"

"Lizzie, will you do me a favour? Don't take this the wrong way, but ... just don't take any more mugs of tea from Cole. For now, anyway."

"What are you talking about?"

"You've been ill after both of them ... it's probably nothing." She brushes it off and busies herself loading the bar up with weights again, but I dwell on her words. Cole – she suspects Cole?

"I think that's me done," I tell her. "I'll wait for you, though."

"Oh, don't be silly. Go for a shower and I'll just have a quick session; we can go back to the dorm when you're ready."

I look around the deserted gym uneasily. "I thought we were supposed to stick together?"

"Lizzie, you'll be a wall away. And anyway, look at all those dumbbells." She points to a shiny rack beneath a mirrored wall by the door to the wet room. "I'm pretty sure I'll be able to defend myself if I need to."

A hot shower does sound good. "If you're sure?"

"I'm sure. We really need to get you back to fitness, though, it'll help your recovery so much. That can be our goal this year."

"If you say so, boss." Kat gives me a squeeze with one arm and pulls me up to standing.

"I do. Now, go and relax. The gym showers are a hundred times better than ours."

"Thanks, honey." I grab my bag and head into the gym shower room, the thought of washing my troubles away spurring me on.

42

I do wish I'd had a chance to plan this one more carefully, but there's not much time left. Not every police officer can be bribed, after all. They're bound to come in the end, asking questions and gathering evidence.

Or worse, the press will arrive. Vermin.

The gym is quiet, which is normal for a Saturday morning, as most students sleep in. Lazy. You don't get to the top by taking lie-ins.

It's so quiet, in fact, she's the only person here.

I watch from the doorway as she does some absurd exercise, lying on the floor and lifting a heavily weighted barbell with her hips. She's in the most perfect position: legs pinned to the ground and her upper body raised up on a bench, facing away from me. I can hear the music thumping in her headphones from here, almost as loud as the shower running in the other room.

There's no way she will hear me.

I trace my fingers along the rack of dumbbells, one kilogram all the way up to twenty-five. I settle for somewhere in the middle, selecting a thick-handled weight. It's evenly balanced, two heavy black hexagons attached by a silver bar. I wrap both hands around one end and swing it through the air experimentally.

That should do it.

I approach her. I'm so close I can see the sweat beaded on the back of her neck, small swirls of dark hair curled around the nape. She's lifting the bar with her lower body, evidently struggling now but still going. I haven't come across a person this determined in quite some time and I feel a pang of something like regret. She could have been quite brilliant.

I wait for her to lift the bar again and raise the dumbbell over my head. As she pushes up with her hips I lower it as fast as I can, the dull thud only slightly less sickening than I thought it would be. Her hands go limp in shock and the barbell crashes to the ground across her hips, pinning her in place. Her head drops back on to the bench and she locks fuzzy eyes with mine.

"It's you," she croaks.

"Yes," I respond, lifting the dumbbell into the air again, before bringing the weight down on to her pretty face. "It's me."

"Liz? LIZ!"

I emerge from the shower with ears full of water and quickly use my towel to clear them.

"Cole?" I start towards the bathroom door and he pushes it open, blocking my path. He looks sick.

"Oh, Liz, oh, thank God." He wraps me in a bear hug.

"What's wrong? Has something happened? Is it ... Taylor?" My mouth goes dry at the thought and he lets go, running one hand over my soaking hair as I try to desperately keep the towel in place.

"No, I mean, I don't know. I haven't heard from Marcus yet. But. . ."

"But what? Cole, you're scaring me."

"Get dressed," he orders, looking over his shoulder and into the gym as I hesitate. "Now! We have to get out of here."

"Why?" I whisper, fear pooling in the pit of my stomach.

Cole closes his eyes.

"Kat's dead."

I can't remember when or how I got dressed, but the next thing I know, Cole is guiding me out of the gym, one hand covering the side of my face to try and stop me from seeing her.

But I do.

There's a gap between his fingers and through it I see my friend, her body thrust back in an unnatural position. Her face is thick with blood and a heavy dumbbell has been discarded next to her. My throat fills with tears and a scream starts to build in the pit of my stomach.

"Come on." Cole practically pushes me out of the door and on to the path between the gym and the lake. "We need to go and find somebody."

"Dr Patel?"

"No." He grabs my arm and starts to drag me along the path. He's twitchy, agitated.

A Cole I've never seen before.

"Wait," I say, yanking my arm free. "How did you

know where we were? School's on lockdown, no one's meant to leave their rooms."

"Which is precisely what you two did." He glares at me before letting out a huge sigh, his shoulders sagging. Behind him the lake twinkles in the morning sun, surreal after what we've just witnessed.

"I'm sorry," I whisper. "You're right, we shouldn't have left. But you know Kat, once there's an idea in her head, she's like a dog with a bone. She doesn't let it go."

"Didn't," Cole corrects me.

Silence drags between us.

"I had to tell you something," he says. "That's why I was looking for you."

"What?" I ask. What else could possibly go wrong?

"It's Patel. I was out on the boys' terrace and saw her walk out into the woods, you know, where we found ... where we found Frank. When she came back she was with that man." My ears prick up.

"Her brother?"

Cole nods his head. "I think so. I couldn't see too well but he looked like the guy she was with the other night."

The cogs in my brain kick into overdrive. All of these deaths and an original cult member back on the grounds – one who has possibly been living *in* the grounds all this time. "Do you really think they're behind all this? I mean, Kat did and look. . ." The sentence sticks in my mouth. Look what happened to Kat.

289

"I don't know." Cole throws his hands in the air. "Liz, this is insanity. There has been nothing but death since I got here and now the one person we're supposed to trust is sneaking an ex-cult member into school, one who has been in prison! What are we supposed to do?"

My mind calms. Kat was the decisive one. The one who put things together. But now I have to do that for her. For all of us.

"We face her," I say, "and we stop them."

"Are you sure this is a good idea?"

"No," I reply.

Cole and I are camped out in the bottom storeroom, one door cracked open so we can see down the corridor to Patel's office. The door to the back stairs is propped open with a huge tin of tomatoes, in case we need to make a quick escape.

"Then what are we doing?" Cole asks, handing me a squashed sandwich. I take a bite, but it's like sawdust in my mouth.

"We're waiting."

It's gone ten thirty, which means that upstairs lights should be out. It seems everyone but us has actually adhered to the lockdown rules, only leaving their rooms to collect the trays of food that were delivered for dinner.

"I think we should just call the police, Liz," Cole sighs, brushing sandwich crumbs off of his jeans. "It's too dangerous. Look what's happened so far. . ."

"We will. Here." I take my phone out of my bag, which is still full of wet gym things, and press it into his hand. "Just not yet. I have a feeling Patel's up to something tonight and if we can catch her in the act, surely that will be better than calling with suspicions. Don't forget, I'm pretty sure she paid off the local coppers. Plus I'll bet she can talk her way out of anything."

Cole sighs. "I guess you're right. I wish you weren't, though."

"Thank you." I lean forward and press my forehead against his. "You've kept me sane through all this, you know."

"Same." He smiles faintly. "How are you dealing? Seriously? I want you to know you can talk to me."

"Honestly, I feel ... numb, I guess?" Is that the right word? "Like none of this is real. I mean, Taylor and now Kat." Her name catches in my throat as I see her battered, bloodied face again. "They were my best friends, Cole."

"I know." He strokes my hands with his thumbs, a soft, soothing motion. "At least we have each other, right?"

"Right." I let him pull me into a hug, his chest strong against my back. I lean back into him and close my eyes.

I'm so tired.

"Hey." A whisper in my ear saves me from the brink of dozing off. "What was that?"

I hold a finger to my lips and push on to my knees,

crawling back towards the door. I can't see much from here but I can see enough.

"Patel is leaving her office," I hiss.

"Alone?"

"Yeah, looks like it."

"Shall we follow her?"

I sit back on my heels and look at Cole. He's so beautiful, even when the world is falling apart around him. I want to keep him safe for ever.

"Not we. Me." He opens his mouth to argue and I hold up a hand. "Stop, I'm not negotiating. I'm going to follow her and you're going to wait here."

"No chance."

"Cole, listen. If her brother is still in her office, you need to follow him so you can warn me." I point to his jeans pocket, where the phone sits. "If something happens to me, I need you to call the police immediately, do you understand?" He opens his mouth to argue again but I lean forwards and silence him with a kiss. "Please? We don't have time to argue."

"Fine. I'm going to check her office and I'm giving you ten minutes, then I'm coming to get you, no arguments."

"That works," I agree. I stand up and stagger slightly, still a little faint from earlier. Cole jumps to his feet to steady me.

"Be careful," he says, burying his face in my hair. "I need you back in one piece" – his lips move to my ear, his breath tickling me – "because I think I'm falling in love with you."

I lift my head in shock.

"What?"

"I wasn't going to say anything, but. . ."

I plant my lips firmly on his. "Shut up," I demand, pulling away. "I think I'm falling in love with you, too."

We take a second to stare at one another before I remember I have something to do.

"Right." I give him one final kiss before I pull the door open and step out into the hallway. "Let's finish this."

44

"I wondered when you would show up."

Dr Patel is exactly where I thought she would be. The library is dark, the only light coming from the security lights that line the exterior walls, but even that's weak in here. Shadows fill the room and I hesitate at the threshold.

"What made you think I would?" I ask, my voice smaller than I would like. I take a step on to the polished monochrome floor.

"Because you're the only one left," she sighs. I walk slowly forwards as she unlocks a glass cabinet with clipped precision, her dark nails glossy even in the gloom. "And you, Elizabeth, like every other Jewel and Bone wannabe, cannot help yourself. The thirst to succeed outweighs all else, am I correct? *Non fortuna nisi per sacrificium.*"

I don't say anything, just walk slowly forwards, glancing over my shoulder at the empty room. Cole said ten minutes. Would that be enough time?

"I know what you're doing." I stop a couple of metres from her, my eyes adjusting to the dark. "I saw your memory box. You and your brother, Harrison, you've been behind everything, haven't you?"

"My brother?" She laughs but it's cold, humourless. "My brother. What a disappointment. You can't choose your family though, can you?" She narrows her eyes slyly at me. "You would know all about that, Ms Williams."

Ouch.

"Oh yes, I am very familiar with your file. As I am with all of your little friends. Taylor – her father is in prison, did you know that? Armed robbery when she was twelve. Real daddy issues. And Marcus, he's not as sweet as he seems, oh no. His son is two now, though I bet he's never mentioned him."

"You're lying," I spit, moving around to get a better look at what she's doing. The cabinet containing the Bernini angel is open. "Stop trying to distract me."

Patel shrugs. "Maybe I am, maybe I'm not. I'll leave you to find out, if they ever return. But you." She taps her chin with one finger, the nail filed to a stiletto point. "You really did have an awful life, didn't you? A useless father figure, a mother who would rather do anything but spend time with you. Never actually neglected you enough for social services to visit, though, did they? Just emotionally scarred you. Made you feel like you'd never be good enough. Well." She pulls open the cabinet door and removes the statue reverently. "We all know what that feels like, don't we, Elizabeth?"

"Is that what your family did?" I say. I need to keep her talking, get her to admit to everything while I can. "Is that why you joined the cult? To show them you were worth something?"

"Joined the cult?" She laughs again and it's a chilling sound. "I never joined that pathetic bunch. They were insane – imagine thinking that killing people would get you anywhere in life. No, I was head girl, the brightest, shining star. I was destined for big things." She places the angel carefully on a nearby table and locks the cabinet again, before producing a long-handled screwdriver. She waves it around as she speaks. "My darling brother put a stop to that, though. My parents were so ashamed. And my name was sullied – no one wanted to help the sister of such a high-profile criminal. Bad for their image, you know? No more sponsors for Nikhita."

"But we saw your brother here the other night." I keep my eyes on the screwdriver and take a step back. It looks sharp. "What did he want?"

"He wanted what he always wants from me. Money.

Somewhere to stay. The only way I can get rid of him for months at a time is to give him what he wants." She pauses, her face a furious mask. "He's very . . . persuasive. He always promises it will be the last time, but as long as he can find me, it never will be."

"So he ruined your life?"

"Bingo!" Patel squeals, her voice edging on hysterical. "My dreams of a shining future were over. I had to scrape a living, training as a teacher, of all things. But I was in it for the long game – I knew if I bided my time a job would come up here and I'd be able to charm my way in as a hard-working alumna. And look at me now." She gestures to her sharp black trouser suit with the screwdriver. Even when she's losing her mind she's still the most glamourous adult I've ever met. "I'm the goddamn *principal*."

"You must be proud of that, right?" I wonder how much of Cole's ten minutes is left.

"Hardly," she sneers, taking her attention off me. She focuses on the small silver lock and pushes the tip of the screwdriver behind it before pulling down on the handle. The lock snaps immediately and the glass around it cracks and splinters. Patel pulls it out and smashes the weakened area with the handle, once, twice, three times, until it shatters.

"Perfect!" she trills, gently taking the statue from its perch on the top. "This way the statue doesn't become damaged, you see?" She stalks over to another case, smashing it, repeating the motion over and over until we're surrounded by glittering, deadly shards of glass. She crunches back towards the table where she had left the angel and smiles triumphantly. Her lipstick has smudged slightly and she has a manic gleam in her eye. "Now that idiot Officer Whipsnade can bring the police in and declare a robbery, like the corrupt little man he is. Once they realize nothing else is missing, that the whole scene was staged, I'll be long gone."

"You're stealing it?" I ask. "The Bernini?"

This wasn't what I expected.

"I think of it more as . . . taking what I'm owed, after I was denied the life I deserved." She strokes the terracotta wing gently. "It was always my favourite. Do you know how much something like this will go for? There are so many private collectors on the black market. My brother was good for that piece of information, at least. He didn't have the balls to do it himself, but I will make millions." I shake my head, mesmerized. "Millions," she repeats, eyes sparkling. "I have a buyer lined up and they have a helicopter waiting for me. Can you believe it? I can spend the rest of my days living the way I deserve to. However. . ." She turns on one spiked heel to face me. "I can't have you ruining all of my hard work, can I? No, I'll have to . . . deal with you."

She's serious.

"You'll never get away with all of this," I say, not taking

my eyes off of her. She's no longer holding the screwdriver and I try to remember when she put it down. Where.

"Oh really? No one suspected anything until you found that picture in my office, you little brat. So now it looks like there will be one more death at Morton before the Principal mysteriously disappears. Boohoo, another head girl – how tragic."

My head snaps up. "Head girl?"

"Yes, you're next on the list, aren't you? A cursed position, in my opinion. Ms Fox is on life support – I've spoken to the hospital, even if she pulls through she won't be back this year. It was a shame about Ms Paphitis, she was a smart girl, or so I thought. So, Elizabeth, that leaves you. The next contender in line." She places the angel down again, looking at it fondly. "We don't want to damage you, my lovely," she croons to it. "We wouldn't want to get any . . . fluids on you." She smiles, turning back to me. "Terracotta can be so porous."

Then Patel's smile fades.

Because *I* am holding the screwdriver.

45

"What are you doing?" Her voice falters as I approach her. Images flash through my mind. Morgan, her face blue and gasping. Jameela, dropping to the ground in her silky pyjamas. Frank, Emily, Taylor. Kat.

I've had enough.

"You said you read my file?" I say, stepping closer. Patel starts to back away and I circle her, the two of us trapped in a macabre dance. "Well, did you? Did it tell you what I did last summer?"

"Yes," she croaks. "You spent the summer in and out of hospital. A head injury you sustained here last July."

"That's right." I turn the screwdriver in my hand. It's

lighter than the dumbbell. "Temporal lobe epilepsy, it's called. It's triggered when someone has a massive head injury, like I did. Causes blackouts, funny turns, that sort of thing. It also causes other ... problems."

"Like psychotic episodes?"

"Not quite." I laugh coldly. "I'm not a cliché, Dr Patel. No, when the temporal lobes are damaged, it can cause personality and behaviour changes. If that happens to someone who is already displaying ... problematic ... behaviour, it can be very, *very* bad. You said you read my file? Liar. You'd have seen my old school was quite worried about my conduct. They couldn't wait to get rid of me."

"I don't understand." Patel is trying to stall me, her eyes wild, looking for a clear path out of the library.

"Well, *doctor*," I mock, "if those symptoms go unchecked for a while, like mine did, thanks to my pathetic parents, it can become a real problem." I play with the screwdriver, watching the dim light glint off the sharpened tip. "I've always had a little trouble deciding what is right and what is wrong – well, by societal standards, anyway." I rap my knuckles on the scar in my hair. "Seems like this just exacerbated everything." I lean in conspiratorially. "I mean, it's not like epilepsy turns you into a murderer, does it? No, I have more ... issues than that. Never actually had a fit, though, so the tablets must be doing something." I look up and see the truth is dawning on Patel. Clever girl. "Who else did you think was killing the students? Your brother? You said it yourself – he's pathetic."

"I . . . I thought he . . . maybe Harrison. . ."

"What, you thought he was providing the perfect distraction for you to carry out" – I gesture at the cabinets – "whatever *this* is? So after all this time, you still thought you were covering for him? Pathetic," I spit. "It was *me*. I read about the cult online. There wasn't much else to do in my summer holidays. And hasn't it all fallen perfectly into place?"

"You're lying, you little witch."

"I'm no-ot," I sing-song. "You see, I never really belonged anywhere," I explain, "until I got here, to Morton. I made sure I blended into the background. I was the *nice* girl, the *reliable* girl. I would have been head girl much sooner if I wasn't playing so nice, if I hadn't helped Taylor and Kat in the Hunt. I gave them the answers. I was so desperate to look *normal*. Then, that night, we took the boat out and Morgan fell in. I really was trying to help her, at first. But I hit my head and when I came to, it was like everything was suddenly clearer. If I could get rid of her, I'd be one step closer. And you know what that feels like, right? The promise of a successful life ahead? I know *you* understand." I lift the screwdriver and point it at her face. "Answer me," I whisper.

Her face goes slack. "You're insane."

I smile. "No. I just stopped pretending to be *that* girl. The girl who lets everyone walk all over her."

"Liz!" Cole's voice echoes through the library and I'm

momentarily distracted. Patel takes the chance to charge at me.

"Cole," I squeal as we both go down, Patel on top of me. "Help me! She's got a screwdriver, she's crazy!"

But she doesn't have the screwdriver, does she?

I ram the weapon up into her chest as hard as I can, aiming for something vital and twisting the end for good measure.

I look her straight in the eye as she lies on top of me. I know she's dying, I can tell. A warm pool soaks out of the wound the sharp tip has made and when the light fades from her eyes, I push her limp body off me and yank the screwdriver out from where it has slid up under her ribs. Even in the dark, I see the bright red arterial blood spray across the room before I drop the weapon to the floor and watch the life drain from her.

"Liz, Liz! Are you hurt? Liz..." Cole drops down next to me and starts running his hands over me, checking for injuries. Creepy Billy is behind him, barking orders down a cordless phone. "Oh my God, all this blood. Are you hurt?" he repeats.

"It's not mine, I . . . I think I'm OK." I make my voice small as Creepy Billy checks Dr Patel's pulse and shakes his head. "She jumped at me and when we fell she..." I stutter, my voice shaking. "She landed on the screwdriver." Cole pulls me to my feet and I look him in the eye. "She was going to kill me, Cole."

I mean, I'm not lying.

"Oh, Liz, I should have come sooner, I—"

"It's OK," I say quietly. "You got here in time." He gently pulls me up and leads me away from Patel's body. "It was her. She . . . she killed them all, Cole." I start to sob.

"Hey, I've got you." He holds me close despite the blood and I imagine what we must look like, silhouetted by the long library windows as red and blue lights start to strobe up the driveway, sirens blaring. "I've got you," he repeats.

"It's over?" I ask.

Cole kisses me on the forehead.

"It's over."

46

I pin the shining black badge to the lapel of my blazer and admire it in the mirror. Head girl suits me.

I still want to grow my hair longer but I've styled it this morning and I'm fairly happy with it. I knew there would be definite perks to having your own bathroom.

I sit on the bed in my room and study the contents of the wooden box, trailing polished fingers over the mother of pearl inlay. I select each of the items in turn, turning them slowly in my hands.

My trophies.

Morgan's photo from that first day, the one I passed to Jameela, her friend's eyes scratched out. I dropped it in the doorway on my way in — I knew someone would pick it up. I was quite pleased to find it in Frank's pocket after I killed him.

Jameela's inhaler and the little tub of Tiger Balm I stole from Kat, most of the contents used.

Taylor's blusher brush: the one I planted the rusty nail in and the little jar of salve I gave her. It smells awful now, the raw meat I mixed in with it has turned rancid. I definitely need to keep the lid on that.

Then there's the almost-empty packet of caffeine pills, the ones I'd been "lending" to Emily. I might have . . . misjudged the dose, though.

The eyedrops I put in my tea, to cause stomach cramps. I couldn't be the only one not affected, could I? That would have been suspicious.

Kat's gym gloves. I've tried to scrub the blood spatter off but that stuff is tough to shift.

I add the picture from the newspaper now — the one of Cole and I walking out of Morton, police wrapping us in foil blankets. We were hailed as heroes, the couple who stopped the Morton Massacre in its tracks.

I'm interrupted by a knock on my door.

I replace the lid on to the box gently and slide it under the bed, smoothing out my skirt and checking my badge one last time. I open the door to see its twin pinned to another blazer.

"Hi, gorgeous." Cole smiles down at me.

"Back at you." I grin, standing on my tiptoes to kiss him. My Cole. Mine, mine, mine.

"You ready to face a new week?" he says, levelling me with a serious stare.

"I think so," I say, glancing at the silver label engraved with 'Elizabeth Williams, Head Girl' on my door. "Only there's just one thing."

"What is it?"

"I want to leave all that . . . stuff behind, have a fresh start."

"Right." He looks worried.

"Not you, silly," I reassure him. "No – I've always hated the name Liz. It's what my parents called me." And they are utter trash.

"You want to change your name?" he says, his brow furrowed though I see the shadow of relief on his face. "Are you sure?"

"Not change it, exactly," I explain. I hold my palm over half of the sign. "Just use a different part of it."

"Beth," he reads, following my gaze. "Beth," he repeats, smiling at me. "I like it."

"Me too." I smile, already visualizing my life as Beth. Liz could stay where she belonged, in the past. The girl with the pitiful family who melted into the background.

"In that case, my lovely Beth, let's go." Cole sweeps an arm out and I follow him into the lounge. He's taken to being head boy just like I knew he would. Marcus didn't come back after Taylor died. Some people are weak. I look up at the new portraits of Emily, Taylor and Kat that decorate the wall, alongside Jameela and Morgan. All those dead girls.

I smile as I follow Cole down the spiral staircase, already

307

daydreaming about our future at Yale together. The governors have agreed it will be all expenses paid, after our terrible ordeal and even though Jewel and Bone has disbanded after the scandal, I'm sure we'll find our way into another society when we get there. It's going to be amazing.

And what Cole doesn't know won't hurt him.

Right?

ACKNOWLEDGEMENTS

In the words of queen Britney Spears – oops, I did it again. Book Two, released mid-pandemic: completed it, mate.

This book TESTED me. I knew where I wanted to go with it, but it's just not that easy to get thoughts from brain to paper – coherently, anyway. It really does take a village and thank God, I had one.

Thank you to my editors, Ruth Bennett, Genevieve Herr, Yasmin Morrissey and Sophie Cashell. Ruth and Gen, you helped me to polish this book within an inch of its life. Thank you. To the rest of the team at Scholastic – Lauren Fortune for believing in my hideous ideas, Jamie Gregory for yet another STUNNING cover, Ella Probert for the most delicious graphics and Peter Matthews for making sure everything was perfect – thank you. Harriet Dunlea – I aspire to your levels of brilliance and organization, you're the best – thank you!

My agents, Stephanie Thwaites, Isobel Gahan and Dierdre Power. Izzy, thank you for all you have done this year, we got there and I couldn't be happier. Sophia MacAskill, thank you for taking such good care of my audio rights and finding them a good home. Thank you to Flora Montgomery for reading my book so beautifully – hearing it was a dream come true.

Thank you to all of the book bloggers, readers and my foreign publishers for making *Last One to Die* such a success. I couldn't have imagined the reception you gave it in my wildest dreams. Thank you, thank you, thank you. To the GoodShip2021 and all of the other beautiful souls I have met in publishing – thank you for your advice, knowledge and support. It's such a pleasure to watch your successes – may they long continue.

To the fantastic colleagues who kept me sane in what was a ridiculous year – you're the best. Sam, Georgina, Sian, Claire, Rebecca, Victoria, Josef, Tracy, Emma. Thank you. I'll miss working with you all but can still annoy you on WhatsApp (and name characters after you, so be nice. . .)

To my two pandemic classes. Online teaching was HARD. However, every morning when I logged on to a chorus of your voices and smiling faces, it made it all worth it. If teaching was more hanging out with you guys and less paperwork, I'd go back in a heartbeat. So, Year 6 Burgundy (2019–20) and Year 4 Navy (2020–21), this one's for you. You might actually be allowed to read them now! P.S. Loli says hi.

Georgia Bowers. You are literally the only person who asks me whether it's too much for a child monster to eat vocal cords. I love our brainstorming sessions (and our moany ones). You are the best and destined to do wonderful things with your writing. Please don't give up. You've got this.

My friends and family. How I wish I had seen more of you over the last eighteen months – hopefully we can celebrate this book together. Emma Bolton (eeek), for your scientific expertise – any gas-chromatography mistakes are definitely mine! Donna, your pride in my first book makes me cry every time I think about it. Thank you. Mum and Dad, thank you for pushing my book into the hands of everyone you have ever met – you are the best parents and cheerleaders ever. I love you all so very much

Loli – I know you can't read (well, I don't think so) but you are the best assistant ever. I'm looking forward to writing my next book in my new office while you bark at people out the window. All the chewy sticks for Loli!

Luke. My brightest shining star. You and Loli have made me smile every single day during this pandemic and I know I wouldn't have got through it (sanely) without you both. You didn't bat an eyelid when I swapped teaching for full-time writing and my heart is ten sizes bigger because of it. You work so hard to provide us with the best life and I am always so, so proud of you. Five years ago, we weren't sure what was going to happen. Now I feel like I'm living my dream. Thank you. I love you, I love you, I love you.

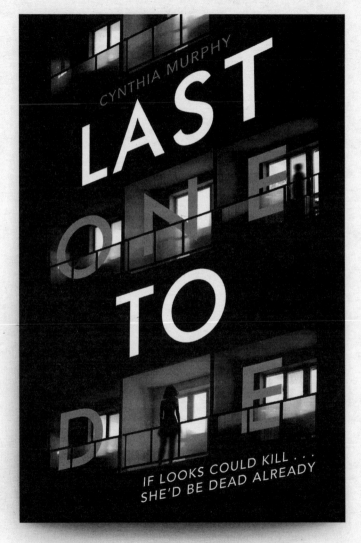

CYNTHIA MURPHY

LAST ONE TO DIE

IF LOOKS COULD KILL . . .
SHE'D BE DEAD ALREADY

"A SUPERNATURAL TERROR-FEST!"
KAT ELLIS, AUTHOR OF *HARROW LAKE*